W9-ALN-121

In the Meantime

Books by Robin Lippincott

Our Arcadia: An American Watercolor
Mr. Dalloway
The Real, True Angel

Robin Lippincott

IN THE MEANTIME

The Toby Press

The Toby Press LLC

First edition 2007
In the Meantime

POB 8531, New Milford, CT 06776-8531, USA
& POB 2455, London WIA 5WY, England
www.tobypress.com

An excerpt of this novel was originally
published in *The Minnetonka Review*.

ISBN 978 1 59264 200 7, *hardcover*

A CIP catalogue record for this title is
available from the British Library.

Printed and bound in the United States
by Thomson-Shore Inc., Michigan.

This book is for Bruce Aufhammer, Kirby Gann, Martha
Harrison, Bradford Johnson and Neela Vaswani

Special thanks to Crystal Wilkinson. And to Lee Salkovitz.
To my sisters and in memory of my father, to Henry Alley, Joseph
Caldwell, Mary Clyde, Eileen Fitzpatrick, Alice Gorman, Joy Harris,
Nikki Louis, Sena Naslund, Louise Riemer, Ray Roberts, Jamie Sieger,
Evelyn Toynton, and Julia Watts. I am also grateful to Yaddo, to the
MacDowell Colony, and to the many friends I've made via Spalding's
MFA Writing Program, as well as to Matthew Miller, Deborah Meghnagi
and everyone at *The* Toby Press.

"In the meantime…(the inviting gesture of dots, dots, dots). Of old, this dodge was the darling of the Kinematograph, *alias* Cinematograph, *alias* Moving Pictures. You saw the hero doing this or that, and in the meantime… Dots—and the action switched to the country." —Vladimir Nabokov, *Despair*

"All the world's a stage,
And all the men and women merely players:
They have their exits and their entrances;
And one man in his time plays many parts…."
—William Shakespeare, *As You Like It*

"Will anyone remember that there were three of us?"
—Anton Chekhov, *Three Sisters*

Before

[Kathryn]

An old man with a mask covering his nose and mouth so that only his eyes are visible; she thinks they were green—or was it the mask that was green? (That is the thing, or one of the things, about memory: it is faulty and unreliable; it can't be trusted). The masked man takes her out of her mother's arms and walks away with her, carrying her—his own hairy arms extended—into a bright white light: she is kicking and screaming, crying, hysterical, her body and face becoming clenched as a red fist in protest; now her mother is crying, too, though less hysterically, but the strange man with the bushy eyebrows and the mask is smiling. She is so young that she cannot yet walk or speak, and of course her fear, if only she could formulate it into thought, never mind words (now it is only a feeling), is that she will never see her mother again—*ever*! And though her mother is thinking the very same thing, but for a different reason, she, her daughter, does not and cannot, know it, because the strange masked man *is* taking her away, and her mother *is* just standing there allowing him to do so.

Separation.

A congenital defect of her infant heart had required emergency surgery. She was less than a year old at the time, and her chances, because of her age and size, were fifty-fifty. The year was 1926.

But if this is her first memory and she can't even remember whether it was the surgeon's mask or his eyes that were green (perhaps it was both?), can she be believed about the rest of it; did this actually happen? And if it did happen, does the true color of the surgeon's eyes/mask really matter?

[Luke]

His mother's dress—a field of small black and white diamond shapes. She is holding him, and as she moves him about on her lap the diamond shapes become smaller or larger or, eventually, a blurry, kaleidoscopic fusion of gray, depending upon his distance from them. He delights in putting a single finger, his pointer, into the center of the light diamond, and then the dark diamond, the light space and the dark space, over and over, and then looking up at her to make sure that she sees what he is doing, and giggling. She giggles along with him—they are united in delight. But suddenly the black and white diamonds grow increasingly blurry, less and less distinct, a gray field, and then disappear completely: she has put him down and walked away, into another room, out of sight. Now it is cabbages that he sees; no, roses (more shades of gray)—a chintz pattern, the sofa. This surface is much softer than his mother, and bouncier, too; he bounces up and down, on the verge of hysteria. Then he hears her voice calling to him; it is muted, faint. She calls his name: *Luke!*

He bounces again. And then again—now feeling buoyant, buoyed, elated: she is still there! She has not abandoned him after all. She is calling his name, signifying him, *Luke! Luke!* and he is laughing and bouncing up and down, so that laughing and bouncing seem to be one and the same. She continues to call his name, over and over, and he continues laughing and bouncing, and then her voice, his name, now one, becomes louder, and still louder, until it is right upon him, and then suddenly she is there, too, and the gray field of her dress becomes distinct black and white diamonds once again, and he is in her lap and can again finger the black space and then the white space, and he and his mother are reunited, together, one.

[Starling]

There are no people, it is people-less, blessedly, peacefully—and only much later in his life ambiguously—people-less, with only the open window and the breeze blowing the sheer flimsy white see-through drapery in and out of the room, sweeping in and then out again, and so on. And that is all, the extent of it, his memory—the frame of the window, the evanescent, blowing, in-and-out drapery, and his own scrawny appendages (arms/hands/legs/feet) occasionally flailing into the periphery of his vision; whatever he can see out the window, through the drapery, or between its panels, is blurry and abstract—*shapes*, is all he could say with any degree of certainty. He must be lying on his back, in his crib, by an open window, and if he could have seen out, he supposes what he would have seen would be a blue sky, or a gray or some other shade of sky (pick an appropriate color) depending upon the weather and the time of day, and green grass, or not green, and maybe not even grass, depending upon the time of year—this could have been anywhere between winter and summer, but he does not recall feeling either hot or cold. He would like to say that he saw a dog or a cat or a bird (especially a starling), or even a quotidian squirrel out that window, but in fact he remembers seeing none of those things (*no white chickens; no red wheel barrows glazed with rain*), for not only is his memory people-less, it is also completely devoid of a single living thing, nary a peep nor a leaf, save himself.

Save himself!

He has been trying to do that very thing ever since.

And he, too—like so many others who have traveled this path before him—has to wonder if this, his first memory, is revisionist, colored by what followed (that is, his life). He cannot say for sure, and that is the troublesome thing.

After

And so Kathryn went—as she did not often, but perhaps twice or at the most three times a year, and always, always at least once in the fall—to the graveside of her beloved friends. *Friends for life*, they had said aloud to each other more than once, and toasted numerous times, over the many years; and yet here she was—old, yes, but still living, though alone; they had both left her so long ago.

The cemetery was outside of the city, in the Bronx (Wood-lawn). She took a taxi there; she had never, all her long life, owned a car. And sometimes she took flowers. Today, she had brought a bou-quet of a variety of blossoms in autumnal colors—rust, red, burnt orange, and amber—which she clutched tightly against the breast of her beige raincoat.

But no sooner was she out of the car than the cabbie took off, peeled off, though she had asked him to wait; it seemed he couldn't get away fast enough; there was a squeal, and even smoke—the quick friction of rubber spinning on pavement. She knew that cemeteries made some people nervous, but this.... *This* had never happened to her before—they had always waited when she asked them to; it meant more money for less work.

Mysterious, she said under her breath with a sigh. But then she shook her head. *Just let it go*, she said into the air. She would figure out how to get back to the city later, when she was ready to leave.

Now she looked up at the sky, which was slate-colored, quickly moving, and seemingly about to open up. Had she gazed at it like that for long, she might have gotten dizzy, toppled over, hit her head on someone's gravestone and ended up with her friends there. But she would not do that—no, she would not do that, because she wanted to go on living, to live; yes, dare she say it, she enjoyed life. And after all, what was the alternative? Not being was, quite frankly, unimaginable to her. Or rather, she could imagine it but preferred not to. She enjoyed her sentience very much, thank you. In fact she relished it, clung to it, like a sailor clings to a ship's mast in a surf-tossed storm—*and what was life if not a surf-tossed storm?*

She eased herself slowly down; the dense, soft, well-mani-cured grass was like crushed velvet against her old knees. She laid the autumnal bouquet in the narrow strip of green between the stones that marked each of her friends. She brushed the stones with one hand and let her fingers slide into the chiseled grooves of the letters in each of their names, which she now fully traced. Then she whispered the sound formed by the grooves, those letters—*Luke, Starling*, each a sound that signified a name, a body and soul; a whole life.

The first drops of rain began to fall....

During

T hey—Kathryn, Luke, and Starling—had always known each other, or so it seemed. They first met at around the age of five and/or six, depending upon which of them you asked, and what month it was (they were all born in the same year, 1925), on the streets of their hometown, a small, nondescript neighborhood in the Midwest where all three of them lived within a four block radius of one another. At that age their memories were still relatively few and unpacked, but their imaginations were boundless.

A wiry girl with strawberry-blonde pigtails and the constitution of a team horse, Mary Kathryn Flanner sprang from a burgeoning Irish Catholic family of three brothers and one sister, of whom she was the eldest; another brother and sister would be born in successive years.

Lucas Aloysius Aldington, whose wide, friendly, and—yes—freckled face, was capped with a bowl of wheat-blond hair, had one younger sister, a ghost of an older brother and a middle name that suggested relatives much further south.

And Starling Torrence, with his startling blue eyes, had neither brothers nor sisters, and yet it could not exactly be said that he was an only child, or certainly not a typical only child, for Starling lived with his mother and one of her two sisters and their mother and several cousins and other relations and semi-relations who were always in and out, coming and going, so that one could not easily pin down precisely how many people lived in the house at any one point in time.

In the Flanner household, Kathryn's mother stayed home with the children but took in sewing for money, always much-needed since her husband Colin could never hold down a job for very long due to his heavy drinking. Luke's mother was also a housewife, but she did not at that time have to take on extra work; things changed for most everyone once the Great Depression fully set in. Bill Aldington was a traveling salesman. And Ermine Torrence did a little bit of everything—hairdressing, housecleaning, *you name it, I'll do it*, she'd say—out of necessity, because there was no husband and father, or rather, he wasn't around, ever: Starling had never met him, nor even seen him, though he knew one thing for sure, not only because his mother eventually told him (that was later), but also (he had known before that) because Starling was nothing if not always hip and he knew a thing or two, and it was this: that his father was white.

And so there they were, Kathryn, Luke, and Starling, in the same neighborhood in that small, midwestern town, in the early 1930s, ages five and/or six, each alone yet in and among their disparate families—and then they met and became somehow bigger, an inseparable threesome; it was a meeting that would transform their lives. And yet none of them could have known then, that innocent summer of 1931, they could not even have guessed, that something as simple and ordinary as a tow-headed boy pulling an already rusting and creaky red wagon with wobbling wheels down a dusty suburban street and coming upon a pigtailed tomboy in overalls just around the corner from his house and asking if she'd like a ride, and the two of them setting off, trading turns pulling or sometimes pushing one another, racing and laughing and screaming down summer's streets, then stopping to talk and generally revel in the leafy June day, and each other, and then before too long happening upon what was *surely*—they both actually said it at the time—surely the *prettiest boy* either one of them had ever set eyes on in their entire young lives, sitting along the side of the road making mud pies and wearing the most elaborate mud headdress, hardening in the sun even as they exchanged their first awkward, monosyllabic words; and then precisely because of his beauty and his strangeness, asking if he'd like to join them—and him, because he was feeling lonely, which, sadly, was nothing new for him, happily and gratefully agreeing; not a one of the three of them could possibly have known then the profound and lifelong transforming effect that this single chance meeting would have (the dominoes fall).

Starling was shorter and skinnier than either Kathryn or Luke, so he stood up; and as he did so his mud headdress—its grains of sand and dirt and clay glinting in the sun, so that it appeared, in flashes, bejeweled—first cracked, then slid, and finally toppled from his head (though he could still feel the hard crust of it drying against his scalp), eventually splashing into the shallow puddle of water he had made with the garden hose.

Luke and Kathryn looked at each other and froze: how, they wondered, would this strange and beautiful boy respond to the sudden desecration of the elaborate and appropriate crown he had spent who knew how long making? His beauty, they instinctively knew, would somehow give him the right to be demanding, to be disappointed, or to be downright distraught (the Boy Diva)—in short, to want what he wanted when he wanted it; and they also knew that now, in response to his ruined headdress, he might very well sulk, or cry, or even pitch an all-out fit.

Suddenly, it seemed that everything had stopped; all was still and quiet—such was Starling's power. He looked at Luke, looked at Kathryn, and ever so slowly rolled his heavily lashed eyes upwards, and then he held them there—this was nothing if not a performance.

He lowered his eyes, looked again at Luke, and again at Kathryn, all of this seemingly in slow motion. And then at last, he threw his head back and started laughing, demonically laughing—those white teeth against the background of what Luke and Kathryn must have thought, if they thought about it at all, was really just a healthy summer tan. And so they, too, knowing it was now safe, joined in, also began laughing, and the three of them jiggled up and down, belly laughing *en masse*, as if they were three marionettes on the same family of strings being manipulated from above—and maybe they were.

I was the King of Muddington! Starling cried, beating his chest.

You still are, Luke told him; you've just lost your crown.

Temporarily, Kathryn added.

Ever efficient, practical, and clear-headed, she was already squatting down onto her haunches and plunging her hands into the mud; her feet were bare, the chipped and stubbed nails painted a fiery red.

We'll make you another one, she announced, gesturing to Luke that he should join her, because this strange and beautiful boy *must* have what he wanted—she felt that; and she could feel Luke feeling it, too: they simply could not and would not have this unique creature, their new friend, being disappointed.

And so they played together through the long, hot, summer afternoon, Kathryn, Luke, and Starling, and by the end of that first day of days they all three knew each other's names, knew where each other lived—Kathryn was just around the corner on Maple and a few houses down from Luke (Elm), and Starling lived three short blocks further down that same long street (typically, Luke was in the middle); and they learned a few other things as well: their favorite colors, for example—red, green, blue; that Star, as he was called throughout childhood, was afraid of snakes; that Katie—an abomination she allowed only up until the age of twelve—knew words like *temporarily* and *abomination* and what they meant, because, she said, her mother *loved* words; and that Luke—not Lucas, and never, ever Aloysius—had an older brother, Laird, who had died recently;

he was nine, and Luke missed him something awful (the red wagon had been his).

And so over the rest of that summer, and on a daily basis, they sought each other out, this threesome—and they found each other, too: it could happen so easily with just the three of them because both Katie's and Luke's siblings were too young to play outside without adult supervision, though they themselves were usually free to do so, and of course Star had no brothers or sisters and so he was always free—*We three free-as-a-bird*, as one of them had once said.

From then on (the very beginning), and unlike most threesomes, there was something completely and wholly equal about their particular three-sided triangle: if Luke and Star agreed about one thing or spent time together on a Thursday afternoon when Katie had to go to the store or run some errands with or for her mother, the next day it might be Luke and Katie who were morally or spiritually or physically together; or Katie and Star. And when all three of them were finally reunited, the two who had been together would make it up to the third who'd been missing by recounting everything, absolutely *everything*—or at least as much as any narrative can capture—that they had talked about and done in the other's absence. Somehow it just worked that way, averaged out, *always*; they were like a jazz trio—piano, bass, and drums—with each player having his or her own say, his or her own moment or turn to contribute and shine in the sun, first individually, and then the two and ultimately all three players collectively, blending and meshing and, all-together becoming one, creating a bigger, better sound.

But Star had this secret, this secret of the two colors, his two colors, or rather of his parent's two colors (he was a *blend*, a third color), though he did not fully know or understand at the time that it was a secret, or even that it was something he needed to be secretive about, though his skin did often feel sensitive; it simply hadn't come up, nor did it come up—until he went to school. And as for how it was that he happened to be living in the same white neighborhood as Katie and Luke, that was simple: his Daddy was a white man—period, end of story. Before Star was even born, the peripatetic and never less than ostentatious Malcolm Torrence had bought the house and moved in, however briefly, with his new wife. Ermine was a light-skinned Negress to begin with, and so the combination of the two had made Star even lighter—like coffee with a lot of cream in it, Ermine liked to say. Almost olive. And so he *passed*.

Sure there were the occasional whispers, especially when folks would see him and his mother out together, say at the market or on Main Street. *Maybe she's from the Islands*, people would say to each other or under their breaths—as if that somehow made it okay with them.

Ermine *was* exotic, even beautiful, on a large scale; the platinum blond and fair-skinned, almost albino-looking Malcolm Torrence had been obsessed with, and loved her only for her melon-like breasts, she would always maintain later: *He planted his seed and then went with the wind*, is what she said time and time again. But Katie and Luke had not yet at that point met or even seen Ermine Torrence, not to mention Star's other relatives, and both friends lived far enough away from him that, at the time, such whispers simply could not be heard from such a distance.

And so this summer was just the beginning of a series, a whole shared history—a life!—of summer times for Katie, Luke, and Star, this one being so very special because their friendship was still fresh and new and unmarked, and because they were learning so much, every single day, about each other and about the world they lived in, as well as about life itself. But they could, they would realize over time, and eventually they did, extend that feeling over a lifetime of summers; it was the long in-between times, the interruption, the very intervention, specifically, of public school, for the next twelve years, that would prove so very difficult for them. Because once they started their elementary education, as they soon would, the usual spoils and banalities ensued: the deadening habit of the droning sing-song tones and sing-alongs, the twenty-six letters of the alphabet and the simple math and the repeated misrepresentations or distortions or outright corruptions of history—the demonization of the American Indian, for example; the quotidian attempts to interject or inject (it *was* like a needle) patriotic fervor—the requisite daily reciting of the Pledge of Allegiance and the forced memorization of "God Bless America" and "America the Beautiful" (a murky mire of church and state); the complete ruination of world literature for so many, through passionless and plodding interpretation and over-interpretation, especially of poetry; the sentimentalization and infantilization of just about everything and everyone—the students, the parents, the teachers (only the principal, in this hierarchy, seemed to maintain his authority and adulthood); and the occasional completely rote or inadequate or even mentally unbalanced, underpaid teacher, not to mention the absolute intolerance of the majority of one's classmates, as well as of one too many teachers, of anything or anyone who was at all unique or simply an individual, i.e. themselves....

But Katie, Luke, and Star, each for her or his own (though overlapping) reasons, and each with his and her own individual style, yet in ways that were both complimentary and sympathetic, were a peer group of three, and they were having none of it, or at least as little of it as they could possibly get away with; but far, far worse was that they were also quite often bored—or so they remembered it all much later. And one of their questions, for the longest time afterward, until other things—other thoughts, ideas, experiences, and other, perhaps more important questions—pushed their way in until there was no longer room to entertain, much less remember, this particular uncertainty, one of their questions, well into adulthood, was whether or not they had emerged from public school relatively unscathed: none of the three of them could ever say for sure, though they all three agreed that Starling had probably been harmed the most.

But to school they went, where they suffered and perfunctorily did their lessons, Katie and Luke more dutifully than Star, who typically could not be bothered, at least not without some extra rousing, such as Ermine's or his Aunt Magnolia's threatened wrath, because Star was usually off in a world of his own making. He certainly could do whatever it was (the lesson at hand) when he needed or wanted (though he never *wanted*) or had to; it was never a matter of his not being *able* to do it, of his not having the intellect or the talent or the wherewithal or the whatever it was that was required for the task at hand—no, that was never the issue; the issue was one of desire, or lack thereof, of wanting to do it or, in his case, not wanting to do *it*, whatever *it* was; and that was precisely Star's attitude toward school: whatever it was, he decidedly and seemingly on principle did *not* want to do it.

Katie's and Luke's parents appeared to have more of an influence on them, or at least control over them, and in this case the appearance *did* approximate the reality. Colin Flanner was a crack storyteller (among many other things), coming directly from Donegal as he did and from a people of prodigious and profligate storytellers, and so Katie liked to listen to him—up to a point. Whereas Mary Flanner was quite simply *in love with the English language*, she often said as much, and had read aloud to her eldest and favorite daughter from the cradle on, especially Shakespeare, and the Romantics: Wordsworth, Keats, Byron, Shelley.... These poems and stories and their language captured and fired Katie's imagination, so that her vocabulary, not to mention the fierce mother-love she got from that kind of early attention (the sound of her mother's voice had become, for her, like the sound of the ocean might be for a child born by the sea), yes, this fierce devotion exponentially increased Katie's ability to make her way through life; her confidence in herself, therefore, and in a benevolent world, was little wonder.

Luke's was the strictest and most regimented of the three friends' homes. His mother's penchant was posture; Priscilla Aldington, with her helmet-like hairdo, looked as stiff as an ironing board when she walked and sat, which gave her an intransigent and intimidating air; and Bill Aldington—who had been in the army and never successfully left it, or replaced it (he had, after all, as he was always quick to remind anyone who would listen, fought in the Great War)—demanded order and discipline of Luke and his sister Laura, perhaps in the magical thinking that he could protect them from the rare and mysterious disease that had befallen their brother. And so Luke carried himself well, made his bed daily and did his homework nightly, but his overlooked heart suffered and pined and was just not in it, not any of it, and he missed Laird terribly. Fortunately, however, he had Katie and Star, friends who fanned and nourished his yearning, burning heart, allowing it to grow and flame alongside his perfect posture and disciplined mind.

And as for Starling—well, he had just seemed to come out of the womb *his own bad self,* as Ermine would always say. There was never much of a question of her, or of anybody else for that matter, influencing or affecting him in any way—except, perhaps, in the way of feminine wiles, but that would become clear only much later...*Star is Star,* Ermine would say time and again, as if that was that. And it was.

And so the three friends flourished and floundered, floundered and flourished, as the seconds and the minutes and the hours and the days, the weeks and the months and the years, piled up and eventually collapsed and got buried underneath the sheer accumulation of time. Those nine months at school—how cruel and preposterous that the academic year had seemingly been designed to equal, in time, the gestation period of a human being from conception to birth, as if the two were somehow on a par, equal—those interminable nine months, out of a miserly twelve in the year—even the clock and the calendar were unjust!—seemed to distort and flatten time to Katie, Luke and Star (especially since, for children, there is *only* the present), and it was for them usually more a matter of flounder than flourish as, irritated, anxious and bored, they tossed and turned, flipped and flopped in their weekday school desks and their nightly beds, like fish out of water. Ah, but during those now sepia-tinted and sun-kissed summers, the season of their first meeting, when they were not, day by day, confined to desks and duties and doctrines—prisons all! Yes, in the summertime their skin breathed, their minds roamed free, their bodies grew and developed and shone in the sun, and their sleep was largely peaceful, dream-filled, and undisturbed.

A frequent refuge on weekday afternoons was Star's house, simply by default—the Flanner household being far too chaotic and filled with Katie's brothers and sisters and her oft-pregnant and already overburdened mother, not to mention the occasional and sometimes volatile appearance of her father, who in those days seemed always to be furious about his growing family (as if he'd had nothing to do with it), complaining to his wife that if they didn't watch out, before they knew it they might have something like the Dionne family situation on their hands; and the atmosphere at Luke's house was much too stiff and regimented, too downright uncomfortable and funereal for that or any other occasion. Therefore, the putrid, sulfuric smell of hair permanents that sometimes permeated the kitchen at Star's house, where Ermine or Magnolia or both *did ladies' heads*, seemed a small price to pay for the greater freedom gained. And so after school the threesome would frequently sit around the round yellow kitchen table at Star's, where Ermine—if she was there, or Aunt Magnolia, if Ermine wasn't there (it was always either/or, if not both)—would give them all, including Magnolia's own kids, Cee Cee, Lavonne and Patrice, each a Coca Cola, and sometimes a handful of peanuts, too, which the three cousins liked to shell and sift into the Coke bottle, then watch as the peanuts fizzed their way to the bottom of the bottle (the shells approximating the color of the palms of their hands), saying that it made both the Coke and the peanuts taste better, and then they, all of them, would sit around that yellow sun of a kitchen table and talk and laugh and relax after yet another tense day in a seemingly endless series of tense days at school, for the cousins also went to school, but to a different one than Star—the one across town for Negroes; all of this while their grandmother, Ermine and Magnolia's mother, Miz Harper as they called her, lay in bed in her shady back room, listening to her radio, fingering the Venetian blinds, and occasionally calling out, as if punctuating the goings-on in the kitchen, or simply having her say, putting in her own two cents, Praise the Lord! Or, Do Jesus!

And so the years, like wheels, rolled blithely by, and summertime always came around again—Katie, Luke and Star had, by now, all three of them, lived long enough to know and feel certain that they could at the very least count on that one thing; and so began the inevitable slow, sly glance toward the future. Yes, this particular summer, the ephemeral *now*, was the beginning of their need to project, a time when the present, perhaps because of a developing awareness of their ultimate powerlessness as children, was no longer enough to satisfy them. And so they raced to meet the future, anticipated acquiring years and experience—and thus also power: what did they, each of them, they would ask one another, what did they want to be when they grew up?

Katie was the quickest to answer: A nurse, she said, because of her mother, who had wanted to be one herself before all of her children came along; it was Mary Flanner who had taught her daughter the value and virtue of serving others—and what greater service was there than that of helping the sick heal? But also, one of Katie's *most* favorite books in the whole wide world at that time was about a very strong and capable girl nurse who saved the day over several far less courageous and competent boys. And at home, over time, what with Colin Jr. and Joseph and Michael and William and Anne and Margaret, and her mother so busy making things run as smoothly as they miraculously did or seemed to do, Katie certainly had, on a small, amateur scale, the opportunity to practice her professed profession, at which both her mother and even her father, when he was around and sober and noticed, said she was a natural.

With Star there was never a question about what he wanted to be when he grew up; it was so obvious—he simply wanted to be what he already was and always had been, only on a much larger scale: he wanted, he said, to be a star, a movie star!

Ermine laughed, in fact she cackled; Magnolia screamed and hollered and slapped her knee; Miz Harper *hissed* her disapproval from her bed—*Sssin-full*; and the cousins—Cee Cee, Lavonne and Patrice—they all cracked-up, too. Tell us something we don't already know, they would say, snickering.

But they also, all five of them—minus Miz Harper, who said she wasn't having none of it—they all treated Star accordingly, because it was just a *fait accompli*.

And for him being a star meant being not an actor or a singer or a dancer or a comedian or any of the other things that might propel one onto that shiny silver screen, not necessarily; no, what Star wanted was simply *to be* on the silver screen, to be known, which is to say that what he really wanted was to be famous, and to be famous for himself—unlike say, for example, Shirley Temple, the biggest box office star of the day, whom Star, Katie, and Luke all three loathed, and they reveled in that shared loathing. She was too cute and cloying—though none of them, not even Katie, knew that word, or its meaning, at the time; it was simply something they felt in their bones: the dimples and the sausage curls and the squeaky voice—it was as if she was a *cute machine*, manufactured to produce a certain desired response in the audience. And that was just it—she was a *product*, a confection of the Hollywood system whose own personality could not and did not override what she had been groomed to be, unlike Judy Garland, who was always just so much herself. And so Star wanted to be famous for who he was, for himself.

Luke was always the most difficult of the three to pin down on this question at the time, probably because he felt that he *should* say that he wanted to be in the army, like his father, or that he wanted to be a salesman, also like his father, though in truth he wanted to be neither. So when his parents would have company over, usually family, for dinner or for some weekend activity (*How about those Cardinals, eh?*), and Luke was asked the now inevitable, unavoidable question, his father would always answer for him while his mother sat passively by, as if somehow oblivious or intimidated—and perhaps she was.

He wants to be like his father, don't you boy? Bill Aldington would boom, after which he would tousle Luke's hair—the only time he touched his only living son, except when he was disciplining him. And what could Luke do but nod his poor tousled head? Whereas when left alone, or with Katie and Star, to answer the question what he really wanted to do or to be when he grew up…. It was…. He wanted to be…. And that was just it: Luke did not know; he drew a blank and could not quite locate what he really wanted to be amid what he thought he was supposed to want. He liked books and read all the time—perhaps he should work in a bookstore or a library?

They were in the bedroom Starling shared with Patrice at the time. The three of them could just fit on the round yellow rug that lay on the floor between the two single beds like a sun; at the end of that floor space was a window.

Maybe you want to be a writer? Katie suggested hopefully, projecting one of her own of oh-so-many desires onto him.

Luke just shook his head: I don't think so, he said, fingering the tassels of the rug. I can't even imagine writing a story, much less a whole book.

Then you should write a story, Katie said, suddenly sitting up straighter, her back against Starling's bed. You should sit down and *make* yourself write a story, over a summer; it would be good for you.

But Luke shrugged his way out of it: he had had enough of doing what somebody else thought was good for him.

You could always come with me, Star threw into the mix, to Hollywood. He gazed out the window.

Hollywood? Luke echoed, incredulous.

Yes, Hollywood, said Star, and then he proceeded to tell Luke and Katie the story of how, when he was younger and first heard the Lord's Prayer—and then for the longest time afterwards, he had thought that the line following "Our Father, Who art in heaven," was, *Hollywood be Thy name.*

But then, beginning in late June of 1937 when they were eleven and twelve, what they had done in previous summers, Katie, Luke, and Star, the fun and the games and the child's play that had occupied and entertained and delighted them for so many seasons, and even present time itself, gradually no longer satisfied. Puberty was just beginning to descend, and the effect of it made them uncomfortable in their own skins, impatient, and even downright irritable at times. All three were also in various stages of feeling sick and tired of their hometown, oppressed by its smallness and sameness and lack of opportunity, and so they began to talk of the future and of moving away together as soon as they could—not running away, but leaving legitimately, after high school, packing up and moving to—*where?*

Once again, they were alone together in Star's bedroom, this time with the door closed, sitting on his bed.

Europe! was Katie's, soon to be Kathryn's, first suggestion—she had read about nurses during the war, stationed in London and Paris. She rubbed the tufts of the chenille bedspread, which seemed to make her excitement all the more tangible.

That seemed too unrealistic, too impossible, unreachable, Luke said, though Star nodded his head and licked his lips enthusiastically, adding that he would still prefer Hollywood—as if they didn't know.

But California also seems too far away, said Luke, though too far away from exactly what or whom he did not say. Then he mentioned the state capital, to which Katie and Star both moaned in unison, making Luke feel just like that fat glass piggy bank atop Patrice's dresser.

New York City! Star sprung on them, with perfect diction and with relish, spreading his fingers on the blue bedspread as if it were the very horizon itself.

The three of them looked at each other: could they? Was it possible—for *them*? Suddenly, a shimmering marquee of dazzling potential was suspended on the horizon and dangled there before them, glittering and resplendent, beckoning: *New York City!*

Why not? Star prodded, kicking off his shoes, I've always wanted to go there.

Me, too, said Katie; and then Luke less convincingly suggested that he had also long been interested in visiting the isle of Manhattan.

We could all live together in a three-bedroom apartment, Katie began spinning the fantasy, looking out the window as if Manhattan were just on the other side.

In Green Witch Village, Luke added, not quite certain of the name but trying to rouse himself, wanting to continue the thread.

And go to the theater and to nightclubs, added Star.

But then in quieter moments, times of solitude, each of them would think about their families. Katie adored her mother with a passion (she knew that she would miss the sound of that ocean, those waves—her mother's voice), and she loved her many brothers and sisters, too—if largely only because of her love for her mother and how much her mother loved Katie and her brothers and sisters. Her feelings about her father, however, were more mixed, because she had seen him drunk and yelling at her mother, and because he was largely absent, even when he was present.

Luke on the other hand did not know quite how he felt about his parents—though he knew that he still needed them, or how he felt about much of anything else for that matter, excepting Laird, and Katie and Star—because he didn't feel allowed to know: *everything* at home was a command.

And as for Star, Star loved his mother and his aunt and his cousins and even his ratchety old grandmother (whom he had secretly nicknamed *Harshy*), but he loved them largely because of the attention they paid him, which was a lot, and when they weren't paying it, or not enough of it, he could and in fact did well imagine living somewhere else and loving himself or, dare he even think it, being loved by someone else.

And so over the next few years, as the threesome embraced adolescence and endured puberty, as they entered and exited junior high for high school, and as they grew and blossomed proportionally and in all of the right places and sprouted pubic hair and discovered, each of them in his or her own time, self-pleasure—Star arriving there first, and then sex, if not actually having it, then at least knowing the basics of how-to, over the next few years, the early teenage years, they were, all three of them, rapidly changing. As if overnight, Katie became Kathryn and would never again accept any other name; she also got her hair cut to her shoulders during this time, a length that she would maintain for the rest of her life. Star eventually grew to prefer Starling, and his preferences were always nothing if not an unspoken demand, though this, too—like so much else about Starling—would change yet again, in time. Only Luke remained Luke, as he always would.

But now school became little more than something to be

avoided or shunned, which they often did, successfully skipping out on at least a part of the day's activities most every single day: Starling was usually the ringleader. Now they would spend time down on the dock at the lake just a few blocks from the school, weather permitting, or crammed into one side of a booth at Johnston's Drugstore downtown, drinking Sarsaparillas or egg creams. Or they would hide out in the stacks of the public library, perusing books about New York City and feeding their fevered dreams.

I have *had* it, Starling was saying now as they sat in one of the booths adjacent to the fountain—walnut wood, heart-shaped mirrors above each one—at Johnston's. Had it with his male classmates making racial comments in his presence (this had been slowly creeping up on him over the past few years, mirroring *their* rising testosterone levels)—comments about *niggers* and *darkies* and their being so dumb or the men being well-endowed, and those boys feeling comfortable doing so around him because they just assumed that he, Starling, was white, or at least not a Negro but *one of them*.

There is *that*, Starling went on, which confused him, because it made him feel happy that he could pass. But then he would immediately feel guilty and berate himself for being glad, because he knew it was wrong, and then he would feel embarrassed and ashamed of himself and inflate with self-hatred. He was also tired of the endless questions, which now seemed to come in a barrage during the first few days at the beginning of every school year, and always, after the first week or so, from new arrivals as well: What was he? Was he an Indian? Was he Greek? Was he from the Middle East? Was he Jewish? Was he an Eskimo? An Arab? Was he from South America? Morocco? Algeria? Africa? Where *was* he from, and what, exactly, was he?

Starling was unsure of just what, exactly, he was—except himself, and *what was a Starling*?

I'm an American, he finally responded—Ermine had given him this one. My mother grew up in Lorain, Ohio, and my father was born and raised in Baltimore, Maryland. It would become his stock answer.

But in his sophomore year of high school, the word somehow

got out about just who—and what—his father was (perhaps Malcolm Torrence had made a wild and sensational weekend run through town in his canary Packard), and who—and what—his mother was, which, so it was deduced, could only make Starling who and what he was, and that was when the trouble really began.

Mulatto, that terrible word—like a freak at the circus or something in a laboratory jar. But also *nigger* and *darkie* and *blackie* and *spade* and far, far worse, because now it was not only words but also deeds, deeds such as boys cornering the always physically smaller Starling in the bathroom at school and shoving him into a stall and then pummeling him with their fists until his nose and mouth bled and his eyes swelled and yellowed and then blackened, until he could no longer stand up or scarcely even see or breathe.

They were especially mad about the deception, they said—*all those years*. As if he'd owed them something more, something better.

Or they would take him to the far reaches of the baseball field after school, on those rare occasions when he wasn't with Luke and/or Kathryn, and beat him up. Or some of them, who could say which ones, put white bed sheets over their heads and then came to his house late at night with primitively made torches, until finally Ermine said that she had had *enough*, and that was it: Marian Anderson had recently taken her stand, that Easter Sunday at the Lincoln Memorial, and now she would do the same, *Malcolm Torrence and his lily-white house be damned*: they were moving to the other side of town to be with their own people, *her* people. But then she had threatened to do that so many times in the past already—why was this time any different?

And Kathryn and Luke were targeted, too, because of their *associating* so much with Starling: *Nigger-lovers. White trash.* And then the barbarian bandwagon began to roll. But it was also during this time that something finally changed in Luke, something broke wide open: because of his love for his friends, Luke quickly and suddenly grew into himself, into his own skin and who he really was, so that now he willingly and eagerly stepped up to the plate and took on the mantle of defending not only himself, but also Kathryn and, especially, Starling as well. By this point Luke was well on his way to the six-feet-plus at which he would eventually top out, and his weight usually ran between one-hundred seventy-five and one-hundred eighty pounds, and his shoulders were broad because he loved to swim and swam whenever he could. Also now, too—even if Luke had nothing else of his father's, or nothing else that he was willing to claim, he clearly had both his father's strength and his sense of honor. And so Luke would do, and did, whatever he could, whatever it took, with all of his might and soul and being, to protect his friends. He knew that Laird would have done the same.

Kathryn's much-practiced nursing skills also came into use now as, like the heroine of her favorite childhood book, she valiantly tended to both Starling's and Luke's wounds after a fight (she often pictured herself, a white cape with a red cross on it wrapped around her shoulders, working under the most warlike of conditions)—the abrasion over a left eye or the cut on an elbow or the ubiquitous bloody nose: first she would clean the wound, then apply Mercurochrome, and finally put on a Band-Aid.

At home, Luke confabulated excuses, saying that this or that injury had occurred while playing sports at school, and his parents seemed both ready, willing, and happily able to accept these excuses, especially since he had heretofore seemed so completely uninterested in competitive sports.

But Ermine Torrence on the other hand was no fool, and she always knew full well just what was happening to her son. Yet she felt powerless about being able to say or do anything to help or protect him—except move, which she finally did do, to the other side of town, to the Quarter, the all-Negro side, bringing Starling and Magnolia and Cee Cee and Lavonne and Patrice and Miz Harper—just as resistant to this change as to every other one—along with her; and the name of the new street on which they found a house for rent, even though it was nowhere near as big or as nice as Mr. Torrence's lily-white house, was, of all things, Mercy, Mercy Street.

But now, suddenly, after so many years, it was nowhere near as easy for Kathryn and Luke to see Starling, or for him to see them—at least not as easy as it had been for so very long, all of their young lives; no, it was no longer a matter of walking three blocks up or down Elm Street and/or around the corner of Maple. Now Starling was way across town; it was a good thirty-minute walk to the Quarter. And Starling went to a different high school now, too, which was, as far as Ermine was concerned, largely *the point* of the move—but then just imagine her having to explain, as she did have to do, just why she wanted to enroll her son in the all-Negro school, when for so many years he had been perceived as white and attended *that* school; but there she was, explaining that very thing: *the proof was in the puddin'.*

So now Kathryn and Luke, most often, or Star himself, upon rare occasion, simply walked the walk, and they walked it, back and forth, every single day, because they had decided that *this*, meaning their valiant and valuable threesome, was inseparable, impermeable, and that it was not going to change—they were not about to let that happen: *they* would not be moved. But what this meant for all three of them, or one of the things that it meant, was—instead of being able to dip in and out of their respective homes, their very own rooms, throughout the course of a long day, to come and go at their leisure—now when they said goodbye to their parents and siblings and/or cousins and left their houses in the morning, they stayed gone until suppertime, and sometimes even later.

And now, too, Kathryn and Luke were spending more and more time over at Starling's place, passing time, sitting around that warm sun of a kitchen table with Ermine and Magnolia and the cousins—or whomever happened to be there—when they had to, or, preferably, fanning the flames of their Manhattan dreams, and listening to jazz records, just the three of them, when they could. Not that the two were always mutually exclusive, however, as Ermine, Magnolia, Cee Cee, Lavonne, and Patrice, everyone in the house, in fact—except ol' Miz Harper, who lay in bed in her darkened back room day and night, her ear to that radio—all of them enjoyed listening to jazz, and they loved dancing, too, just as much as Kathryn, Luke and Starling did, so that sometimes it became nothing less than a full-fledged, flat-down, drag out, and fun-loving party.

Yes, a real party, where Ermine would close the door to Miz
Harper's room and get the second-hand Victrola out from the closet,
and then begin to spin so many records so fast that a person both
could and would get dizzy, and before too long Magnolia would
become *Mags* and soon she could be found pushing aside the throw
rugs with one foot, and then sooner rather than later they would all
jump in—moving furniture and turning down the lights and beginning to feel so high-spirited that they would laugh to beat the band—
until the place was as it should be, which is to say dance-friendly, and
then the dancing and the singing and the carrying-on would begin,
slow to catch on and patchy at first, but then growing—over time—
and swelling, as the hour grew later, until things were really jumping, hopping, happening and swinging, to Louis Armstrong doing
his own "Sweet Georgia Brown" or "Dinah", or Billie Holiday singing "Miss Brown to You" or "Your Mother's Son-in-Law" or "What
a Little Moonlight Can Do", but then somebody, usually Ermine or
Magnolia, one of them would inevitably slow things down, down to
a thick, heavy slowness that felt like so much poured molasses, they'd
slow that rhythm down to something such as Bessie Smith dragging
that old ball and chain around through one of her blues numbers,
moanin' *oh! oh! oh!*, and this was when most of them would pause
and take a break and wipe the sweat off their faces and necks—and
sometimes further down—and reach for a cold drink (and by now
some of the neighbors may have come over, too, and joined in),
because they were not at this point in their lives, any of them, save
for Ermine and Magnolia, particular fans of slow dancing—though
Kathryn did nurture a secret longing to slow dance with *just* the
right man, and Starling carefully tended a flame of an illuminated
fantasy of him and Luke out there on the dance floor together, holding onto each other and dancing close and slow; but then before too
long somebody would change the record *and* the tempo by putting
on, say, Django Reinhardt and his Hot Club of France as they fre-
netically sped through "I Got Rhythm", or "It Don't Mean a Thing
if it Ain't Got that Swing", and the place would start jumping again,
literally jumping and jiving—Django's fast-strumming guitar setting

the quick pace and getting the heartbeat and the blood pressure humming and thrumming to his and his hot quintet's frantic, rapid, rabid rhythm (a hummingbird playing the guitar with its wings, someone had once described Django), and then usually the cousins and Starling and whatever neighbors there were—because this was something they did *all the time*, and later Kathryn and Luke, too, would get up and dance, jitterbugging and fox-trotting and you-name-it, spinning and throwing and swooping and scooting and swaying, wildly and hectically and also, quite often, improvisationally, but always, always full-tilt and with abandon until, eventually, that particular song would come to an end and then it would seem—suddenly and for the briefest of moments, yet a moment that had an impact and lasted—suddenly it would seem as if the world itself had also come to a quick end right then and there (and sometimes lately, especially because of the surprise attack on Pearl Harbor, sometimes it seemed that it *had* or soon would come to an end), because now there was no sound and there was no movement, after there had been *so much of both*, and then they would all look at each other, really look, at each other's faces and into one another's eyes, until it seemed that some moment of truth was about to occur; but then the next song would begin and the body would just take over once again, seemingly with a life of its own, and the jumping and the jiving would resume, and at some point, Kathryn, Luke, or Star, one or two or all three of them, would make the analogy, would say that dancing was like their summers together, wasn't it?, with the rest of the year, the school year, being that time in between songs when there was no music and no dancing, and the other one or two would nod and say *Amen!* And there was a kind of truth in that, too, someone else who'd overheard them would say, because music *is of time*, and it *marks* time—through assonance and dissonance and rhythm and repetition and lyrics, however artful or organized or not (there is no metronome in jazz), and so on and so forth, free form, free form—bee-bop-a-doo-lop-a-dee-a-tri-la-la-la-la-la, schweeeeeeeeeeeee....

And so the years passed, they just swung by, accompanied by and inviolately intertwined with music, and music was nothing but a freight train, a large barge barreling down this track or that river with its incessant and inexorable and indefatigable rhythm, leading our fearless threesome on, pulling them along body and soul—the sweet umbilical c(h)ord of sheer momentum, and then propelling them forward toward the future and eventually hurling all three of them out of their small and respectable but-just-not-for-them midwestern hometown, and on their way to…. But not yet. No, not yet, because they were, still, only sixteen and seventeen years old, and they had a couple of years of high school left; but also, the fierce struggles in Europe and beyond had exploded onto the world stage and into an all out, white hot, world war; and it was now, and for some time to come that seemingly just about everything in their small lives began to break down and fall apart, mirroring the world in precisely that same way.

Meanwhile, down at the lake, Kathryn, Luke and Starling, on yet another school day, and during school hours, sat on the dock dangling their feet in the water; and because they were, all three of them, not doing much of anything other than listlessly complaining about this and/or that—there was, as they saw it, so much to find fault with at this time in their young lives: school itself, their peers, their teachers, their parents, their siblings or cousins, their clothes, their hometown, *the world!*—wise Kathryn, surely the most sagacious of the three at that time, suggested that they all three recall, or rather she asked that each of them recount, their very earliest memory.

But only what you can *really* remember, she added. No cheating!

There was silence at first, as if they had, all three of them, been caught up short and heard themselves as they had been for the past however long period of time, whining and complaining; they had become self-conscious, embarrassed and ashamed of themselves.

A flurry of birds sounded off from across the other side of the lake as they suddenly scattered; a remonstrance or response?

A fish broke through the glassy surface of the water, puncturing the perfect mirror-table, breaching ripples.

And then it was Luke who began, and *this* was something they had long done and enjoyed, this sort of round-the-room response to whatever one of them happened to lay on the table at any given time.

I was sitting on my mother's lap, he said; she was wearing a dress with a black-and-white diamond pattern, and laughing.

Kathryn smiled and said, That's lovely, and Starling smiled, too, but his was a sad smile, a brief, evanescent rise then quick fall of his facial muscles, so that the smile seemed to turn down at the corners of his mouth almost as soon as it had been seen—not at all the bright headlights one was used to from Starling.

Now a bird, perhaps one of the same flock that had sung or sounded earlier, soared across the surface of the lake, swooped down, then dove, ducked its head underwater—briefly, but with a precision that reminded Kathryn of the tango—and then just as quickly re-emerged, with a small fish in its beak: was it, could it be, they asked, the same fish that had, moments earlier, disturbed the glassy surface? Was there an order to the universe after all?

Life goes on, Luke said, as the three of them watched.

My mother put me into the arms of a strange man wearing a mask, Kathryn began; she had been waiting. I was crying hysterically—kicking and screaming; I was about six months old at the time and the man was a surgeon; this was for the heart problem I've told you about. And because he was wearing a mask, all I could see were his eyes and his bushy eyebrows, and that made him, and the whole experience, all the more scary.

Gosh! Starling said.

Luke just gawked.

And Kathryn then laughed a laugh of relief, letting out life's very air, because here she was—she had survived and was fine. And as a result she suddenly wanted to deflect the attention away from herself, and so she turned to Starling and, with an expectant, inquisitive look, said, Your turn.

But Starling didn't particularly want to recount what he remembered.

It's really not much, he said now to his friends, who continued to look at him impatiently, waiting.

It's just me in my crib, looking out the window.

He glanced at them, hoping they might say that he could stop then and there, that he didn't have to go on. But that same expectant, inquisitive look that Kathryn had shown earlier was now on Luke's face as well.

And so Starling reluctantly began: A see-through curtain blows in and out, and either through it, or in the gaps between the two panels, I'm not sure which, I can see the sky, and I can see, in the distance, the ground. And sometimes I can also see my arms and my hands, or my legs and feet, superimposed over whatever is in the background. He paused, shrugged, and then he looked at their blank and clearly still-expectant faces. He could see that they wanted more; they were disappointed, he knew it. But there was no more, and so he told them:

That's it!—no conflict, no drama—no one else in the picture.

And there was that same, sad smile again—Kathryn saw it; and then she resolved to relieve Starling's pain by quickly changing the subject.

Let's talk about New York City, she said suddenly, and what we want our lives there to be like! She would have clapped her hands together, invoking enthusiasm, had she been that sort of person, but because she was not, she did not, and instead, Luke picked up her cue, came to the rescue and ran with it, suggesting that they buy a map of Manhattan, and perhaps also a travel guide, and actually begin making plans, real plans about *when* they would make the move and *how* they would do it and *where* they would live and *what* they would do, both to earn a living but also with their free time, for fun, because the wonderful fact was that they already knew the *why* (or thought they did), and oh, Luke began to wax poetic, We have so much to look forward to!

Now Starling perked up, and the look in his eyes at that moment, just after Luke's venerable call to action, could very well be said to typify or characterize his mien over the next few years—*focused*;

driven, as he was beyond ready and willing to do whatever was necessary to leave, to go; yes, he was ripe—all three of them were. And
suddenly the years, indeed time itself, seemed to fly unexpectedly
by, perhaps because now their eyes were so firmly set on that very
specific horizon, that prize, which they vigilantly kept in their sights
like a pilot does a runway. And so now, too, it seemed that almost
everything they did was toward that one end, that one dream—that
horizon, those runway lights—of landing in New York City together,
and then *spending* their lives there.

But alas there were still classes and peers and parents to be
reckoned with; school dragged on and on, and making things worse,
patriotism, that friend of nationalism and distant neighbor of xeno-
phobia, now—because of the war—was in full hue and cry. Kathryn, Luke, and Starling, at their respective schools, skipped out on as
much of the hoopla as they possibly could, which was only *so much*,
after all; and they did, all three of them, at least once, and Starling
more than once, get caught—it was usually that one old librarian,
the heavily powdered and bewigged Mrs. White, who found them
out and told, and then they were inevitably sat down and spoken to
by one or both parents.

Kathryn's mother, at least, was understanding: her daughter
had long ago confessed to her that she was bored at school; and from
the sound of it, Mary Flanner said, it was little wonder—*practically
spoiling literature for her daughter; making even Wordsworth seem dull!*
And yet she knew, too, that even bad teachers couldn't completely
dampen Kathryn's enthusiasm, thanks to her own language-love and
her always fervent ministrations on its behalf. And Mary was also
aware of Kathryn's plan to move to New York City with Starling and
Luke, because Kathryn told her everything; and though she wasn't
exactly thrilled with the idea—*New York City; living with two men*—
a part of her was proud of and excited for her eldest and favorite
daughter; and yes, there would be something vicarious in it for her
as well, and she would not, no she would not, she steeled herself, do
anything to hold Kathryn back; she trusted her implicitly.

The Aldingtons, however, were appalled to learn of Luke's

truancy. Priscilla Aldington actually used the word, arching her stiff back—Appalled—at such behavior from a child of hers!

There would be consequences, Bill Aldington took over, malevolently fingering his belt buckle. Consequences, young man. Cause and effect—a full week of coming home immediately after school, coming home and staying put, no lollygagging with your friends.

So Luke served his time, and he got through it easier than he otherwise might have done with the help of Kathryn and Starling, who visited him at his bedroom window at night several times during the week, while the elder Aldingtons, sitting in the living room listening to Arthur Godfrey on the radio, or entertaining neighbors or relatives, were oblivious, just as they also knew nothing whatsoever about their son's New York plans.

And Starling's mother? Not yet forty years old, Ermine Torrence was simply *worn-out* from her son's dodge—Star was what he was and always would be, and she had learned long ago that there was and would be no getting in his way or stopping him. Take this crazy idea of his of moving to New York City with Katie and Luke, for example: All right. Okay—sure, you just go right on and head out along Route 66 with your self! She'd look forward to visiting him there; she had long wanted to go on up to Harlem, a trip Malcolm Torrence had repeatedly, time and again, promised her they would make, early on. We'll just see if it happens, Mister Man, she would conclude every discussion with Starling on this particular subject, because she didn't, and she didn't because she couldn't, quite believe that it *would* happen—her boy in New York City!

And then something happened all right, and though it was certainly nothing even close to what Ermine had in mind, something occurred that would almost prevent Kathryn, Luke, and Starling from ever realizing their dream of moving to New York City together; and that something was so big and powerful and primal, so disruptive and divisive, that it did postpone the move for well over a year. It was in the waning months of their junior year of high school, spring 1943, with only twelve and a few more months left to go—and three of *those* summer months, before they were free. But it was also one of those times when the cards are just stacked in a certain way—as will happen, one of those instances where the stars, as it were, are lined up; and yes, it *was* also spring, and that fever is an undeniable force (it was, as the song goes, *just one of those things*). This particular thing happened on a Saturday night, when Kathryn, unusually, had to stay at home with her younger brothers and sisters, because their mother suddenly had to go to Cincinnati where her eldest and favorite brother, Kathryn's Uncle Jack, had been found dead on the street; he'd had a problem with alcohol for years. Mary Flanner knew that she could not confidently count on her husband to stay home and watch the children, and that if he did stay home, she couldn't be sure that he would be sober.

Just around the corner, Luke's parents, along with his sister Laura, were out of town for the weekend—a state beauty pageant in the capital city at which Laura was a finalist (but, alas, *only* a finalist, much to Priscilla Aldington's ire). The threesome's plan for the evening, therefore, was this: Starling would show up at Luke's between seven and seven-thirty, and from there they would go over to Kathryn's to keep her company for the evening. But Starling had something else in mind—yes, he had carried this particular torch for a long, long time, and so he had plotted.

He arrived at Luke's shortly before seven-thirty, as planned, but he arrived with a bottle of wine, a rosé, he called it—never mind how he got it, that was easy in the Quarter—and Luke had never before drunk wine and was definitely curious. So Starling uncorked the wine in Luke's bedroom—even the shape of the bottle was pleasing; they would go over to Kathryn's soon, after a glass or two, and surprise her with what was left, he said. And then the two began to drink.

Luke liked it, he said, at least after the first few minutes; it took some getting used to: initially, the wine had tasted sour, or bitter, but then somehow *how* it tasted became more complicated over time—it was difficult for Luke to explain, more enjoyable and fruity and, well, *intoxicating*; and he liked it. And before too long Starling had poured each of them another glass, and time passed, and then another, as they stood there talking and laughing, just being their

43

usual old selves, standing there—surrounded by all of that oppres-
sive dark wood in Luke's bedroom, with Laird's side of the room
untouched, intact—talking about Hitler, of all things, laughing about
his moustache and how it looked as if some furry insect had taken
residence above his upper lip.

At some point the telephone rang, sounding distant and muf-
fled in the other room, but Luke *didn' really wanna answer it,* did
he? Starling asked. It wasn' nothin'. And then after the third glass
of wine, Luke, smiling and even laughing slightly, his lips plump
and purpled, said that he needed to sit down, because the room was
spinning and he thought that maybe he was getting dizzy, plopped
down on his bed.

*Starling immediately eases down beside him, takes Luke's face in
his hands, and kisses him long and hard and with his tongue; Starling
has been practicing on his cousins.*

*At first, Luke protests, puts both of his hands on Starling's chest
and sloppily and thickly-tongued says, Ssshtar! and tries to push him away.
But Luke is weakened by the effects of the alcohol, his reflexes are con-
siderably slowed down, and the feeling of Starling's tongue in his mouth,
touching and intertwined with his own tongue—all those awakened and
sensitive taste buds!—is pleasurable, is enjoyable; Luke has not yet even
done this with a girl.... And also, he is tired, and the room is spinning,
and so he slowly lowers his torso, and then his head, onto the bed, the
innocent bed with its massive mahogany headboard and its cowboys and
Indians bedspread that has been his and that he has known and slept
in and lain on to read and contemplate the world for such a long, long
time, for as long as he can remember, and that he has thought of in a
certain way, only now it no longer feels like that same bed, but different,
like something else, like a boat on the water—something less solid; or it
is like his parent's bed and the feeling he gets whenever he lies on it, and
yet it feels good, too....*

And then the next thing Luke knew for sure, that he really
remembered with any kind of clarity, was that there was now a faint
light in the room that had been darker, and he felt someone else's
skin against his own, and it was Starling, naked, lying in *his* (Luke's)

bed next to and up against him, and his (Luke's) mouth was so very dry and his head hurt something awful; and then he remembered, he remembered at least some—*enough*—of what had happened last night. It was the proverbial morning after, a new day, and things would never be quite the same again, *ever*, and a terrible reckoning was to be had.

Luke moved slightly so that his and Starling's naked bodies were no longer touching, then he glanced over at Starling—his dormant head was turned facing Luke; and finally Luke looked, really looked at his lifelong friend—the long eyelashes fanning out into the shadowy valley made by his high cheekbones; the surprising Roman nose; the full lips pursed in sleep.... Starling was still the same person, Luke reminded himself, and he was also, all these years later, still that same prettiest boy that Luke and Kathryn had ever seen. But then Luke emerged from his reverie: he could not forget what had happened. He felt dirty and ashamed. Starling had essentially seduced him. And he, Luke, was simply *not that way*, nor had he known that Starling was. And he would have to tell Starling, and this could never happen again, *Never!* And as Luke heard himself saying the word *Never!* in his mind, his anger at Starling suddenly grew: Starling had taken advantage of him. He had no right. He had violated their friendship. And now Luke jabbed Starling hard with the sharp bone of his elbow and quickly sat up, careful to cover his nakedness.

Starling, he said, in a clipped if somewhat hoarse tone as he saw his clothes strewn about the room; he got up and quickly dressed.

Starling, wake up! This time Luke kicked the heavy bed.

One of Starling's eyes opened. Then the other. A half-smile crossed his face—the sharpness of Luke's voice had not yet registered—as he began to prop himself up on his elbows; but then he couldn't support his head and he let it fall back into the pillow.

Hey, he said, innocently sweeping toward Luke with one *paw*, all softness and fuzzy, happy thoughts.

Luke stood over him now, scowling. I said get up!

And then Starling knew, he just knew—this time he clearly heard the tone and volume of Luke's voice, and it registered, and now he had his response to the unanswered question that had hung in the air between them for so very long, almost a lifetime; he remembered what had happened, or some of it, and now he knew that Luke remembered it, too; but what he knew most of all was that what had happened between them the night before, and more importantly what he had done, had not gone over well with Luke, not at all, and now, now all he could think of was that there was surely going to be *hell to pay*, Ermine's expression. And all the time, too, really just moments, though it seemed an eternity, all the time that those thoughts were registering with Starling, Luke was standing over him, his arms crossed, a scowl on his face, and there—a tear! A tear sliding slowly down his cheek.

Why? was all Luke said when he finally spoke. But then he let out a volley of screams, a profusion of *whys*, over and over, louder and louder, so that he sounded like some bird, or a whole flock of birds, at hazard.

I love you, was Starling's simple response.

Luke kicked the bed again.

I'm *in love* with you, Starling corrected himself, or continued, and at this Luke visibly flinched.

And it was then that Luke finally said it, told Starling that he was not *that way*, and Starling nodded, as if accepting Luke's statement; but then he asked if Luke hadn't enjoyed it, because he knew, in the way that one lover knows about the other, he just knew that Luke had taken pleasure; and Luke, though he did not give voice to it, felt confused, because it was true, he *had* enjoyed it. But he was drunk, he reasoned, and besides, he just wasn't *that way*, and he kept on intoning the phrase, and repeating it, over and over, not only because it was true, but also because he couldn't possibly bring himself to say the word, the word that defined *that way* (he had often heard his father deriding *those people*), and the way that Starling apparently was. There was so much for him to be angry about, Luke said—*what* Starling had done and *how* he had done it, but also that Starling hadn't, long before last night, told Luke that he was *that way*, he'd thought they were best friends.

Suddenly, he had another thought. Luke demanded: Did Kathryn know? He sat down at his desk and reflexively put the dictionary on his lap, as a shield.

Starling shook his head. He was stunned. And hung-over. He wasn't sure what he had expected, but it wasn't this; no, it was not this. His own scenarios, which varied in the particulars, all had in common the very vague notion that he and Luke—and Kathryn, too, of course, though in another respect—would move to New York City and, essentially, live happily ever after.

Kathryn, Luke said, remembering: We abandoned Kathryn last night. His stomach flipped; it felt as if his intestines were performing somersaults. Please go home now, he said, turning away. I can't…. I don't want to see you—for a while.

Starling climbed slowly out of the bed and began dressing, Luke's back turned to him the entire time; then, just as soon as he could, he left the house and started that long walk home.

Kathryn, meanwhile, had naturally been worried about her two friends—that had been her calling on the telephone—especially after all of the harassment they had received over the past few years, so that when she eventually learned, later that same day, that Starling and Luke had been together at Luke's house the entire time, and drunk!—but that was *all* she learned—she became furious: why couldn't they have at least let her know, told her they wouldn't be coming over? This was the first time that she, or any of the three of them, had been intentionally excluded, and she was deeply hurt.

And so the threesome dispersed for a time. But Kathryn could stay angry and hurt and away from her lifelong friends for only about a week before she had to reach out to them again, and yet she was the one who had to extend a hand first, and even then she could only meet with each of them separately, as both Luke and Starling refused to see her with the other; Kathryn knew and understood *nothing* of what this was about, nor would they tell her, and so for the time being, she told herself, she would merely focus, with each of them, on repairing the damage that had been done with her. But that was relatively easy to do because, like her mother, she was a forgiving person, not one to hold a grudge, and also because now there was this much larger issue, this elephant in the room, of Luke and Starling refusing to see or even speak to one another, and her knowing nothing of that, though she had begun, privately, to guess what it might be about. And then she asked, directly asked each of them, if what she had been thinking, which was that something sexual had occurred between the two of them, was in fact true, but neither would answer her—though Luke's averting his eyes, and the unusually *set* expression on Starling's face, she thought, was an answer of sorts.

Assuming that she was right, Kathryn understood. She understood because she herself longed for another, someone to love and to lean on. Luke and Starling were like brothers to her. And most other boys her age were so silly and immature; and then if they grew into men like her father—well—no, thanks. She would wait until she was older, wait for a mature man, one who was comfortable in his own skin.

And then along came summertime, another summer—the season of their first meeting, *their* season, and the very last one before the summer of what they had for so long thought would be their emancipation, but Luke and Starling still would not see or even speak to each other. And so Kathryn continued to get together with each of them individually, and things were just beginning to feel relatively normal between them again, as normal as they could feel with one of the three always missing, which is to say not normal at all. And now the joint move to New York City was no longer spoken of. They had tried, early on, Kathryn and Luke, Starling and Kathryn, to talk about it, but it had not gone well—how could it? And so an unspoken moratorium on the subject had finally settled in. Kathryn, however, was not one to give up, not that easily, and so she continued, over the days and weeks, to work on and away at Luke and Starling, trying to break them down, until finally she managed to convince them to meet, first just the two of them alone, without her, on the dock at the lake, on a Saturday morning late in August.

That day started off hot and humid, so that by eleven the temperature was already hovering near ninety degrees. The plan was that

Luke and Starling would meet first, at noon, to talk things through, and then Kathryn would join them at one o'clock or so, bringing along a picnic lunch for all three. But by the time she arrived, intentionally fifteen minutes late—walking slowly down the sandy path that led to the dock, expecting to find Luke and Starling talking together, even laughing, like old times—it appeared that little to no progress had been made whatsoever, as the two sat on opposite sides of the dock looking out at the water. It was such a desolate image, and all of Kathryn's hopes for the day, and somehow for the future, too, were immediately deflated, and suddenly she felt as limp and lifeless as the very air that all three were breathing. Perhaps she could sit between them and be the glue, the magnet, that brought their threesome back together? But no, that was not to be, not today anyway. And so the afternoon went: Kathryn could only do, could only effect, so much, she realized then; and they ate their picnic lunch, those who ate at all, in virtual silence. It was awful, terribly awkward, perhaps even ruinous; all three of them were miserable, and before two o'clock they had left the dock separately to walk home alone.

And then along came September and their final year of high school, a time that should have been a happy one, full of hopes and plans and dreams for their future together…. But the fissure in their threesome continued, as Luke and Starling still would not see or speak to one another, and they, all three of them—out of sheer necessity, not because they wanted to—began to plan a future that did not include the other two, or at least not necessarily. Kathryn and Luke went to the same school and so saw each other frequently without even trying, though they did also try; but now that Luke was not available to walk across town to and from the Quarter with Kathryn—especially at dusk, or later, she could not make the trip as frequently as she had; and because Starling was unwilling to make the trip very often for fear that he might, accidentally, run into Luke, which would simply be too painful, Kathryn and Starling no longer saw each other as often as they once had, and now an even greater chasm opened up in Starling's life, one that he would have to fill.

Thus their senior year of high school began inauspiciously,

though in a matter of months now, they, each of them, would be released, freed, finished, would have come through, just as they had long anticipated; but then what? Their parents had, that fall, been asking each of them this very same question, and telling them that they should be asking it of themselves as well: what were they going to do after high school and, for that matter, for the rest of their lives? Such pressure!

Starling, oblivious to what was going on in the world at large, as usual, still held his own private dreams of leaving the area and becoming a star, and he knew that even to begin to realize those dreams, he would need money. And so he planned, he told his mother, to get a job in Riley's shoe store—because he knew someone who already worked there, and because he loved shoes and figured he'd be able to get them for free.

Ermine laughed, and informed him that shoes were among the many things that were currently being rationed—or hadn't he noticed?

At which point Starling surprised even himself by taking a job as a waiter in a downtown restaurant, working after school and on weekends.

Luke, his father had told him, would naturally serve his country, as soon as he came of age: there was a war going on. Period. There seemed to Luke to be no question about this, none whatsoever, at least as far as his father was concerned (his mother appeared conflicted, divided between worry over her son's well being and the desire to support her husband and country)—but Luke found himself questioning it nevertheless. Draft be damned.

Kathryn began acquiring information about the state colleges—there were two, filling out the necessary forms, and then applying to both. Moving to New York City was simply not an option for any of the three now; none of them had the heart.

If he was going anywhere, Starling told his cousins, it was to one place and one place only, and that was Hollywood. And Kathryn was either going to one college or the other, both within the state. Whereas Luke, poor Luke was not sure where he was going, if he was going anywhere at all, or just what he would be doing, because in truth—so he confessed to Kathryn—he did *not* want to serve his country, at least not in that way, as a soldier: he was frightened; he did not want to die young.

And so the school year passed, and much precious and valuable time was unconsciously and unintentionally wasted. Kathryn spent more evenings at home with her mother now than she had in years; and often, after her brothers and sisters had gone to bed—her father was usually out late, at the neighborhood bar with his cronies—she and her mother would read aloud to each other. Most recently, Mary Flanner had been reading from her beloved Wordsworth:

A slumber did my spirit seal;
I had no human fears:
She seemed a thing that could not feel
The touch of earthly years.

No motion has she now, no force;
She neither hears nor sees;
Rolled round in earth's diurnal course,
With rocks, and stones, and trees.

The poem clearly had to do with the all too swift passage of time, and the death of a beloved. Had her mother chosen to read this poem for a reason, Kathryn wondered? Was she trying to tell Kathryn something? She looked at her mother's face now and thought she had her answer as she watched a single tear slide from the corner of her mother's eye, run over her cheekbone and down the side of her jaw.

Take nothing for granted, Katie, Mary Flanner said, turning her face in an attempt to hide the tear. And yet, you have to keep going, too, keep moving forward.

By the end of the school year, Kathryn learned that she had been accepted at both schools. She chose the one in the state capital, closest to home, and for now at least—she reserved the right to change her mind later—much to her mother's pride and joy, she would major in English.

Starling arranged to begin working full-time at the restaurant; he was rarely home now, because in addition to working so much, he was also—in order to fill the gaping hole left by the absence of Luke and all that the dream of Luke had meant to him over the years, and sometimes even as an extra source of income—sleeping with strangers, multitudes of strangers.

Whereas Luke had been engaged in a fierce, year-long battle with his father, and more silently with his mother: he did not want to, nor would he, he finally screwed up the courage to tell them, enlist in the army; he refused.

You what? His father had hit him the first time he said it, reflexively punched him in the stomach, and they had gone back and forth all year long, until summertime came and Luke, still only seventeen, graduated from high school and his father finally gave him an ultimatum: either Luke enlist in the army immediately, or he move out of the Aldington home; it was that simple.

Luke moved out, rented a room in a boarding house, and got a job in the library shelving books.

The summer passed in a haze, and suddenly it was September again and the leaves began to fall, and now what Kathryn, Luke, and Starling had done for the past twelve years, and almost always done together, which was to go, however reluctantly, to school, they no longer *had* to do; but Kathryn had chosen to continue her schooling, and off she went—her mother's words echoing in her mind, *You just have to keep going, Katie, keep moving forward*—though not without first seeing and saying goodbye to Luke and Starling, both of whom, she thought, looked sad and had lost weight; and the season had a falling feel to it, a spiritually downward and melancholy slant, and it seemed to Kathryn now, despite her genuine excitement about college, that she, Luke, and Starling had fallen from grace in some way, and that it was a grace that they had wrongly taken for granted; but of course she could see that only with the perspective of time, in hindsight, and her question to herself now was—could they ever get it back?

From her dormitory room at school, which she shared with a roommate (not someone who would become significant to her, but a nice enough girl), or at one of the study tables in the high-ceilinged library beside an emerald-green-shaded reading lamp, where she wrote her papers and sometimes scrawled poems in the margins, Kathryn also wrote letters to both Luke and Starling, though only Luke responded.

She loved his letters, which seemed, as she told him, to replicate his speaking voice: he had that talent. He was reading a lot and enjoying it, he wrote, and he was thinking that perhaps eventually he could do something with it, maybe something in the publishing field. Kathryn wrote back encouraging him, also telling him that she at least liked *some* of her classes, especially Shakespeare—Professor Lawrence was brilliant; but most of her classmates were another matter. She missed him and Starling *so much*, she added; there was no one like either of them; she especially missed their threesome.

Kathryn saw both Starling and Luke on holidays and vacations: Starling apologized for not answering her letters; he just wasn't the letter-writing kind, he said, but he enjoyed receiving hers. And Luke told her that he liked working in the library; he liked the books, of course, but also the quiet, the peace, which was so unlike his parents' home. He said that he had not seen them, his parents, since he'd moved out, though he had, secretly, seen his sister Laura.

His life now was simple and he said he liked it that way, for the time being. He got up, went to work, came home, ate dinner, and read. He read, and he thought. Most importantly, he was on his own time schedule: sometimes he went to bed early, at ten, if he felt like it, and got up at five or six the next morning; but at other times he would stay up well past midnight or even later, and then sleep as late as he possibly could, until just before he had to leave for work. And meals were anytime he wanted, and anything he wanted them to be, though so much was being rationed at the time.

Starling's life was much the opposite: he was *never* at home, except to sleep, and not always even then. Nor was he often alone, quiet, or still, but always on the prowl. Strange men came to the house now upon occasion, looking for him; and more than once Starling had come home late at night with a black eye or bruises on his face.

Waiting up for him just especially one particular night, Ermine sat Starling down under the harsh light bulb that hung over the yellow kitchen table and told him that she didn't know exactly what he was up to, but she sure didn't like the looks of it. She wagged and pointed her finger and told him he was selfish, that he should be ashamed of himself:

There's a war going on, son, she said. People are suffering all the world over.

Starling just sat there, his head lowered.

He had best be careful, she went on, and mend his evil ways.

Of course her gravest concern was that he would be sent over there to fight. Wouldn't it just be so ironic, Ermine thought—her people finally getting the vote, Starling coming of age, and then him going off and getting killed in the war. Because if she knew anything at all, it was that her boy was not a fighter.

Starling looked just to the side of his mother the entire time— silent, fearful, and exhausted. But she appeared tired, too, he had to admit; and it was because of him: he knew that he owed her more, and better than he was giving her.

I'm sorry, he said with a question in his tone, mindful that it wasn't enough, not when she wanted him to change his very ways, which he felt powerless to do: if she only knew what he had been up to.

Ermine Torrence looked long and hard at Starling, then rose from the table saying, quietly, It's late; let's go to bed. And then she hugged her only son like she hadn't hugged him in years, tight and full of meaning—as if she could squeeze the evil ways out of him, wishing she could protect him, keep him safe with her love, yet knowing otherwise.

And then one day in mid-April, a month or so before Kathryn was due to arrive home for the summer, Starling and Luke ran into each other, one street over and across from the library; the biggest surprise of all was that it had not happened before now. Luke saw

Starling first and stopped in his tracks, which caught Starling's eye. There was so much feeling, then, in that moment of their seeing one another for the first time after so long, a flooding of blood to the heart and mind. Luke smiled. That was a good start, Starling thought, and he smiled back. They approached each other slowly, cautiously.

Hi, Luke said, immediately shoving his hands in his pants' pockets.

But Starling could not speak; he had clinched his jaw in an attempt to keep his emotions in check. And then he spoke and said what Luke had wanted and been needing to hear him say for so long:

I'm sorry.

Luke squeezed his eyes shut to hold back the tears.

Me too, he said.

Each of them thought that the other looked changed, different—thinner and sadder, but also grayer, less healthy.

And then Luke added: I miss you, and now Starling could control neither his smile nor his tears, and he extended his right hand—his impulse was to hug Luke but he thought better of it—and Luke took Starling's hand in his and then covered it with his other hand, and the two of them stood there looking into each other's eyes, shining for all the world to see.

And then they actually talked, chatted—walking along slowly, past storefronts and passersby, *lost in the moment*—not that either of them could much remember afterwards what the other had said, because they were both so stunned by the sheer fact that they were facing each other and talking once again, after such a long time. But talk they did, and most importantly they made a plan to meet and talk further; but they would not tell Kathryn, they agreed, wanting to protect her just in case things didn't work out: not yet.

That next meeting happened just a week later, over dinner at a friendly neighborhood restaurant in the Quarter. Sitting on red leather seats in a booth, a dimly lit lamp on the table between them, Luke immediately ordered wine—because they could, here. It was a gesture not lost on Starling, who began by apologizing again and saying, repeatedly, that what he had done was wrong and that he knew that now; he could promise that it would never happen again. But then he added, lowering his voice, that Luke should know that it was true, that he, Starling—now he was whispering—was a homosexual.

Luke nodded his head—of course he knew that now. He said that he had done a lot of reading and that he thought he could separate himself from other men, the same men, he added, who had discriminated against Starling for being half-Negro and half-white. And he said, too, that he thought he understood. But in turn, Luke went on, Starling must know that he, Luke, was not homosexual. And with that now out of the way, they could and did move on to discussing other things—Kathryn, their lives, separately and together, how it felt to be out of school; and eventually it seemed almost like old times again, so that they were also finally able to talk about their threesome's dream of moving to New York City together....

We should surprise Kathryn when she comes home for the summer, Luke said, which was only a few weeks away now. We should just show up at her house together and surprise her.

Unbeknownst to them, however (she had not written in well over a month), Kathryn was suffering during the final weeks of the semester: how much the news of their reunion would have helped her!

Now she begins composing a letter, to Luke—which she neither finishes nor sends:

(undated)

Dear Luke,

I wish there was a telephone in your building so that we could talk right now, because I really need to talk to you, now. But in lieu of that I am writing to you, which is the closest thing I know to talking with you, being with you.

I'm not sure what is going on with me. It is school, the end of the semester, exhaustion, studying for my final exams—yes, it is all of those things;

but it is also just the state of the world. It seems that I spend most all of my time worrying—about the war, about my family—especially Mother, and about you and Starling.

I am so exhausted and now I have not slept for days and days. Maybe an hour here or there but not much at all and I fear that it is beginning to catch up with me. I am feeling a little crazy, you know? Nor have I been eating well; I just can't stand the thought—it almost seems wrong, when so many people are suffering; I'm not even sure that I could keep anything down.

I had no idea that all of this would be so stressful—school, being away from home. And I've got some crazy professors, too, which doesn't help. Did I tell you, I can't remember, I don't think I did, that my poetry professor (Coleman) won't let us study the haiku, because of the Japanese! Isn't that crazy? Not only crazy but scary, too. It's insane. And then there's my British lit. professor, dear, eccentric Professor Stein, whom I genuinely like, and admire; he knows and clearly loves Yeats at least as much as my mother does. But instead of reciting poems like "The Lake Isle of Innisfree", he trenchantly reads "The Second Coming" ("Things fall apart; the centre cannot hold...") over and over again, and then he goes off on these rants about the terrifying goings-on in Europe. (Don't you think it's really strange that President Roosevelt died, and Hitler committed suicide, all in the same month?) And none of this is helping me at all, not at all, because I'm just so worried all of the time, and it seems that the world is falling apart, and that I am falling apart, too—crumbling, a mere crumb, slowly and gradually dissolving, disappearing

August 6, 1945

[Seichi]

*I*f only my earliest memory—that golden globe of fruit hanging from the gingko tree outside my window, whole, full of promise and seemingly impermeable, like the sun, or like the world itself—if only it could have held as a true representation of the world...

The morning broke clear and warm; I was at the temple, as was my custom at that hour. At around 7:30, there was the usual air-raid siren, a minute-long blast—a sound we had grown accustomed to hearing in those days: it blared every morning when an American weather plane flew over and was supposed to indicate only the slightest degree of danger. I noted the sound and looked up into the sky, as usual, and then I went on with my daily prayers, just as I had done countless times before.

But then at 8:15 the whole world changed, and it changed forever: an American plane dropped the first atomic bomb on Hiroshima, Japan. For some time afterward, unable to imagine the truth, people were suggesting that it was gasoline that had been sprinkled from an airplane, or a *Molotoffano hanakago*—a Molotov flower basket—which is the delicate Japanese name for self-scattering cluster bombs. We simply did not know what had hit us. All we knew was the blinding flash we experienced—some of us saw it as white, others saw it as yellow, or golden; one described it as a *sheet of sun*. And someone else said that it looked as if the sun and the earth were melting together. But almost no one who was there and close-up recalls hearing anything at all.

Then such clouds of dust arose that I could scarcely see or breathe; and of course there was the ominous giant, mushroom-shaped cloud itself, the *kimoko gumo*, like a huge, evil head, which hovered over Hiroshima, more or less intact, until the following morning, at which point the shape began to change and amorphize.

The day grew suddenly dark, it was like twilight, and the cloudy air gave off a terrible thick smoke. Once we were able to clear our eyes, those of us who were still standing, which is to say still alive and not seriously wounded, what we saw, gradually, were the fires, the orange flames licking multitudes of houses, and we saw, too, that so many buildings had collapsed, some with people trapped under them and with just their legs sticking out. Others had been cut in half. So many buildings had been destroyed that those few still standing only accentuated how many had fallen, how horizontal and flattened everything was. Buildings that had been on the banks of the Kyo River were now *in the river*. The wind suddenly picked up, too—far more fiercely than in a typhoon: I saw people literally pulled apart by it.

I remember first noticing that the golden statue of the solid and honorable Buddha had crumbled and been reduced to rubble, and then I saw that the heavy fence at the temple had fallen on several people, most of them young girls who had been taking rest beside it. They were trapped underneath. I could not lift the fence alone, though I tried repeatedly. I called for help—*Tasukete! Tasukete!* Help! Help!—but no one came. Then one trapped girl, probably sensing her fate, invoked our Emperor, Hirohito's name, and began singing *Kimi ga yo*, the national anthem, and the others soon joined in.

Gambare! I heard someone, somewhere, call out. Be brave! And they *were* brave, all of them, singing *Kimi ga yo* over and over. But other than helping them to be strong, affirming their love of country, and distracting them in their time of great pain and distress, their bravery did them little good, as they all died anyway, trapped there—all but one girl who somehow managed to find a crack in the fence and get out. And she is Hara Midori, who became my friend, and who lives every day burdened with the knowledge that she survived and her friends did not.

Eventually, through the thick clouds of smoke, I began to see all the people, hordes, throngs, a whole horrible sea of people, so many people—three-fourths of the population of Hiroshima was either killed or wounded on that day; people swollen and naked, or in shreds of clothing or bloody underwear; people charred and crawling through the debris like animals; people whose hair stood on end. On some undressed bodies, as so many were, burns from the heat of the bomb blast had made patterns—undershirt straps, suspenders, and the like; silhouettes of men, women, and children were burned into sidewalks as they walked or fell, and shadows of objects, such as ladders and shovels and cranes, were imprinted onto the sides of buildings. Some people's eyebrows were burned off, and skin hung from their faces and hands; there were children with hollow eye sockets, the fluid from their melted eyes running down their cheeks; and so many people, *so many people*, were screaming, running and screaming at the same time, as if the two were somehow connected: *Itai! Itai!* It hurts!

Mo dame da, Mo dame da. This is the end!

I reached out to take the hand of one old woman to try to help her, to comfort her, but her skin dropped off and she slipped out of my grasp. There were stories of people throwing themselves into the River Ota to cool their burns, and of their skin coming off and floating on the surface of the water; and many people were vomiting uncontrollably now, too, running and vomiting at the same time.

I saw several mothers carrying their dead children in their arms or on their backs, unwilling—or unable—to let go. I saw so much that day; I saw too much, and I think, for awhile, I somehow lost sight of everything, and that I went, literally, *out of my mind*: it was all far more than one's brain could hold; beyond comprehension. Others describe this as well, a kind of shock I guess it was, a shock and then a total shutting down of the system. Because we saw too much: I saw things that no human being should have seen or ever have to see again; I saw things that I, a poet, a man who loves words, have no words for; things for which I believe there are no words.

And I was one of the lucky ones; I was all right. I had many cuts from flying debris, and a few abrasions from having been thrown down with the initial blast, but I was not seriously wounded. I was alive; I had survived. And that was one of the strangest things—among so many strange things about that day: you would see huge structures completely demolished and made rubble of, and then you would see a paper fan or a scroll or something equally delicate, something made of papier-mâché, perhaps, that was left whole and intact. One of the most incongruous things I remember seeing was a billboard advertising Lion Toothpaste, suspended in a tree. Suddenly, nothing made sense anymore, and it must have been then that I realized that nothing would make sense for a very long time to come, if ever again; things as we in Hiroshima knew them—and in the entire world, too, I would argue—had effectively been turned upside down.

Then, something happened that we could not understand at the time, only afterward, which was true of so much about the event and the day—though there are things that I and many of us will *never* understand: very large drops of water began to fall. My immediate response, and the response of so many around me was to cover our heads with our hands, those of us who still had hands, and run for cover. It was not rain, the scientists later explained, but drops of condensed moisture, falling from the volatile column of dust, heat, and fission fragments that had risen high into the sky over Hiroshima.

And all the while those of us who were able to help were trying to do so. I, along with many others, was so very worried when the metallic rumble of a B-52 sounded over our heads: what would happen next? Would there, at any moment and without warning, be another tremendous flash, and then the same horrendous after-effects?

It was possible. We couldn't take any more. We were all terrified. But doing something, simply acting—aiding the wounded, helping where we could—quieted those fears somewhat, and helped to free us from our own terror.

We carried so many people to the Red Cross Hospital on make-shift stretchers fashioned from bamboo and straw rope. The hospital itself had been damaged by the blast, though not destroyed. There, the staff, too—the doctors and nurses—had been damaged, so many of them killed or wounded, but some had survived. And so those who remained worked around the clock for days; it was later said that by nightfall on August 6th 1945, one hundred thousand people had gone to the Red Cross Hospital for treatment. But it was also there at the Red Cross Hospital that I gradually began to see or to hear about—or worse, *not* to hear about—people that I knew, people I loved, who had either been killed or badly wounded. My parents were all right, I somehow knew—they lived in Mukihara, thirty miles from the city. But I lost my beloved cousin Yutaka—and his parents, my aunt and uncle. Even worse, my older brother Isawa, my parents' only other child, we learned later had also been killed. His remains were never found or identified, he just disappeared, and so of course we knew. And then later, months later, some unidentified person wrote to us that Isawa had probably been killed instantly because of his proximity to what was determined to be the center of the explosion, which explained why there were no remains.

I lost so many relatives that day, along with former classmates, acquaintances, and friends, including my two best friends—Fukai Yukio and Murata Myeko, whom I had known since childhood; we had grown up together, had gone to the same school. What can I possibly say about them? That they lived, for nineteen and twenty years, respectively; that they were good friends, lifelong friends (I knew them for fourteen of those years); that they were, both of them, good people, and that they had hopes and dreams and plans, just like the rest of us. All of that is true, but it is not enough.

Myeko was a nurse at the Red Cross Hospital; she was so proud to be a nurse. Ever since she was a little girl, that had been her aspiration, her dream, her mission, even. She had played nurse with Yukio and me all through the years when the three of us were growing up; and then she had worked so very hard to become one, denying herself and sacrificing so much in order to become this person who was trained to help others.

Myeko was a very small person—short and thin—and yet her mind was strong and fierce. She could have easily become a doctor and maybe would have in time, had she been given that opportunity. But she always had a laugh ready, too—she was not overly serious; it was there, just behind her twinkly, intelligent eyes: how I used to love to make her laugh! Especially at the most inappropriate times, and in the most inappropriate places, such as in class.

We shared so much, Myeko and I—all of the things that children share over time: fun and games—how we both hated the daily calisthenics at school, always performed to lively music!—and learning and petty jealousies and silliness and boredom and excitement and maturation…. And now all of that is gone, because she is gone, though I still have my memories, which are now in some way *our* memories.

Ironically, and very sadly, on the day of the bomb Myeko was not at work. She had just left home—her parents' home, which was situated near the River Ota; she was still living with them. It was 8:10 in the morning and, unusually, she was running late—she had been helping her mother clean up after breakfast; she was on her way to the temple; on her way, in fact, to meet me. And she had so many errands to run that day, her mother told me. The only thing we were able to learn is that she was found dead in the middle of the road somewhere between her home and the temple: her parents told me that the kimono she was wearing at the time had been burned off by the blast, and that its pattern of flowers—pink peonies against a white background, her mother said—had been imprinted upon her body, which, as I have said, was petite.

I want to leave you with her body.

Fukai Yukio is another story, another loss, just one of so many, of hundreds of thousands, but one of *mine*: he was my best friend.

Yukio was a soldier, stationed at the Chugoku Regional Army Headquarters in the center of Hiroshima. He was tall for a Japanese man—a head taller than I and most, and he had broad shoulders, too, like a swimmer, which in fact he was. Yukio had just turned twenty less than a month earlier, on July 16th. We had celebrated—with Myeko, of course—at a restaurant in a building beside and over the water of the Kyo River. I remember that night so well—Myeko's eyes, full of intelligence and glee, and Yukio's laughter—he was so very happy about turning twenty, becoming a man: I gave him a paperback about a samurai, a topic about which he always loved reading. And I remember, too, that a full moon was hanging in the sky that evening, and also shimmering on the surface of the river, reflected from above. Yukio commented on it; the fact that something as solid and real as the moon could appear to be so watery and insubstantial—*like my early memory of the ginko fruit, I think now, and like the sun, like this world*—and Myeko knowingly said that all things were relative.

But despite the fact that Yukio was twenty and becoming a man, he was, for the most part and in so many ways, still a boy. I know because I, too, was still a boy then, and Yukio was my best friend—the bombing of Hiroshima caused me to grow up fast. Yukio was a boy who just happened to be in the army—a very ancient and very sad circumstance that happens all the time.

Ironically, that day, the day of the bomb, Yukio was with a squad of soldiers from Chugoku Regional Army Headquarters who were burrowing into a hillside, making one of the many dugouts that were intended to be useful in the case of an invasion. Yukio was among those soldiers who were actually in the hole at the time of the blast, instead of along its periphery. He and the others in the hole *should* have been safe. But that was not the case.

While I was working at the Red Cross Hospital that first day and night trying to help out, amid everything, among the many things I overheard, some of which were untrue, mere rumor (rumors were flying that day), was one doctor telling another that a large number of military casualties from the Chugoku Regional Army Headquarters had been transferred to the Military Hospital on

Ninoshima, a nearby island. *Yukio*! I remember thinking about him in that moment—where he was, if he was safe—but I was so totally engaged, so caught-up in the moment, that I could not think about him for very long, no more than a few seconds really, and also keep my mind on what I was doing, which was—essentially—whatever I was being told to do, mostly applying rags immersed in soybean oil to the burns of victims. And so both Yukio and Myeko, that day and for a while, had to be placed into a far back corner of my mind, where I could only hope that they were safe.

Two or three days later, I am no longer sure which, after I had worked myself into exhaustion and then collapsed and slept for more than fifteen hours, I was able to think, once again, about Yukio and Myeko. I learned about Myeko first, simply by visiting her bereft parents. But Yukio had no immediate family in Hiroshima or close by, and so remembering what I had overheard about some military casualties from the Chugoku Regional Army Headquarters being transferred to the Ninoshima Military Hospital, I went there. Their records, miraculously, were very good and well-kept—probably because it was a military hospital, and also because it was wartime: Yukio had been admitted on August 6, 1945, bleeding profusely from the neck—a scrap of metal, perhaps a piece of a shovel sent flying through the air from the blast, had lodged into and severed his jugular vein. By the time he arrived at the hospital, there was little that could be done other than to try and comfort him as he lay there and bled to death, but there was no one there to comfort him, everyone was helping someone else; all was chaos.

And so I leave you with his long and once strong body.

A favorite haiku:

> In the depths of the flames
> I saw how a peony
> crumbles to pieces.

> —Kato Shuson

Hibakuska is a Japanese word that means those who have seen hell, and I am one of them, one of the many, though so few of us lived to tell of it. I am Sato Seichi, and my body, my *very body*, not just my mind but *my body*, buckles and folds under the weight of all of those other bodies, until I feel that I will collapse from the weight and the heaviness and the sadness of all of those bodies—the bodies of my brother Isawa and my cousin Yutaka and his parents, and of course, the bodies of my best friends, Yukio and Myeko, and of so many other relatives and classmates, and the bodies of those poor schoolgirls trapped under the fence at the Buddhist temple, and so many more, all of the bodies of Hiroshima, and the bodies of Nagasaki, and all of the bodies of Tokyo, and the dead bodies of all of Japan, as well as all of the American bodies and the German bodies and on and on, so many bodies, mountains of bodies, the bodies of war…until I feel that I cannot survive. And yet here I am—I survive.

Just in time

[1]

When they—Kathryn, Luke, and Starling—finally land in New York City that fall, their arrival is not announced in the press, but it might as well be, or so they think at the time: *At last!* Yes, at last!—because it seems as if there has been so much for each of them to overcome, individually and collectively, so many obstacles, before they were able to break free from and fully escape the shackles of their small, midwestern hometown, both its mindscape and its landscape, board a train called *The Pacemaker*, and then, less than twenty-four hours later, arrive not only in the midst of a seemingly mythical Manhattan, but also into the million dollar mouth of nothing less grand than Grand Central Station itself.

The train finally comes to a complete stop and the threesome, alongside so many rote commuters, uninterested businessmen, addled tourists, beloved infidels, and a few hopefuls like themselves, begin to disembark. All three of them have by now, aged twenty or twenty-one, assumed, in appearance, who they are and will more or less remain.

Here is Kathryn, of average height and weight for a woman of her time and place. Her face has the shape of an upside-down triangle, nicely framed by shoulder-length, wavy red hair, which has darkened to a cinnamon color by now. She is not beautiful but pretty, and there is a wisdom in her hazel eyes and across her high forehead that makes her appear more than merely pretty, but also smart and strong-willed.

Next off the train is Luke—a fully-grown man now, and a strapping one at that; he tops out at just over six feet and has the shoulders and the body of a swimmer. His hair is still blond, if slightly darker than the sun-kissed color of childhood summers, and his face—always a kind face, with those clear, sky-blue eyes and apple cheeks—remains full and boyish; in short, Luke looks much like the midwesterner that he is.

And the last to emerge onto the platform (perhaps because he is making an entrance?—this is, after all, his New York debut) is Starling, still the same *prettiest boy* that he was at age five. He is not much taller than Kathryn, and he is slim, his body perfectly proportioned. His curly black hair is on the short side, and his face is still smooth and free of any trace of stubble; his doe-like, long-lashed blue eyes and his bright smile are what most people notice first.

These initial snapshots taken—and captioned, perhaps, *The Happy Travelers*, or *Home Sweet Home*, or more simply and to the point, *At Last!*, the threesome stand on solid New York City ground for the first time, together and with their bags at their feet, their mouths agape, and then they naturally gaze upward.

It looks like a beautifully ornate, delicately wrought bowl, Kathryn says, all of the muscles and veins in her neck and face straining in that domed direction, like a sunflower toward the sun. A bowl made of iron lace, then turned upside down. She grabs hold of their hands and says, Let's just stand here for a minute and take it all in.

Sunlight is pouring into the building, and there is such a hustle and bustle of people around them, throngs of people buzzing, coming and going, commuting to and fro, people on missions (they are sure of it)…as the three of them stand there, completely still, almost sculptural (a frieze), fully in the midst of it all, soaking up that particular sun.

It almost seems, Kathryn says now, as if we might hear a choir breaking out into rapturous strains of *Gloria in excelsis deo* at any moment.

And Starling will later acknowledge that it had been this very instant when he finally knew for sure that they had realized their dream—or one of them.

And so the threesome moves through those early days in Manhattan assembling their lives, both individually and collectively, as if their movements are choreographed, each with his or her own known and well-rehearsed role, each part fitting together into a whole, and all of it adding up to a dance performance worthy of Balanchine or Graham (whose companies they, in their excitement, have already been to see perform in those early, heady days).

First, they find a venue for their lives—on the fifth and top floor of an old brick building at the corner of Amsterdam Avenue and West 110th Street. It is a railroad-style apartment, long and narrow, like a train car, which, Starling says, is perfect—since it was a train car that brought us to the city in the first place. Thus, where they live, he goes on, will symbolize both the connectedness and the continuity of their journey. I never want to *arrive*, he adds finally, as if arriving is the worst possible thing.

The front door of the apartment opens onto the living room, which leads into the long hallway, off of which are—first, the bathroom, and then, three bedrooms, one right after the other; and at the end of the corridor is a large, eat-in kitchen, with an outside door that opens onto a very small back porch (Starling likes to say that the *Divine* cathedral—St. John's—is their backyard). Thus the stage is set for living.

And those early days in the city are indeed exhilarating, as the threesome soon realize that the summers they had so revered and reveled in as children can now be spread, like so many preserves, throughout the entire year, that is, that all of the seasons can be like their childhood summers, because now they are all three together, living together, in New York City, and because they are making their own decisions, running their own lives, instead of always reflexively responding to the demanding and deadening drumbeat of their parents or their schools or the mind-numbing thrum of habit itself. And so they decidedly do not march to anyone else's drum in those early days, but rather they dance to their own music—they waltz, they fox-trot, they swing—to a cacophonous and carefree city symphony, to a jazz downbeat, because in those days, as long as you were in the mood, and especially if that mood was indigo, it didn't mean a thing if it didn't have that swing, and man oh man did it ever have that swing, then. And so imagine each of them, Kathryn, Luke, and Starling, first as a single groove on a 78 LP, and then picture them and their experiences, individually and collectively, doubling and tripling and quadrupling and so on, over time, so that as the world continues to spin 'round and around (if not exactly evolve), and as the days become weeks and the weeks add up to months and the months, eventually, tally to years, and as those years pass, the grooves that the trio have been laying down are continually intersecting and coinciding, blending and meshing....

And that meshing produces, among oh so many things, a bohemian menagerie—our *salon*, as Kathryn likes to call it—of secondhand furniture and colorful knick-knacks (the *accoutrements* of their lives); an overstuffed chintz sofa and mismatching armchair, several director's chairs, a couple of bookcases, a phonograph, three beds—two twins and one queen-sized, and it is anyone's guess who got the queen!—a red, gold-flecked Formica-topped kitchen table and several mismatched metal chairs with different colored seats and backs. All of the walls in the apartment had been painted an innocuous off-white, but just months into the occupation and already those walls are overly full-to-bursting with colorful paintings in differing sizes—some well-known prints, some originals, as well as scarves and baskets, and, in the kitchen, multiple hanging gadgets, such as a potato masher, a rolling pen, a spatula, and the like. Thus the trio can begin playing out their new lives—seeing the sights and sounds—and the shows, and generally making the scene.

With the help of a scholarship (and near-perfect grades), Kathryn has transferred from her state university to Barnard College at Columbia, just a stone's throw from where they are living, and where she has now also secured a part-time secretarial job in the English Department. Luke quickly gets a position in publishing—working in the mailroom at McGraw-Hill. And Starling, for the time being, is living off the savings from his job in the restaurant back home, and just beginning to go on auditions.

[2]

I f you could do anything you wanted today, Kathryn asks now, anything at all, what would it be?

Sitting at the kitchen table on a Saturday morning, she looks relaxed in dark slacks and one of Luke's unpressed white dress shirts, a cup of coffee in her hand. It is newly spring, when the leaves of the trees are still that fresh, light-green color, and the forsythia bushes and the Japanese magnolia in the neighborhood are just beginning to bud and blossom.

Across from Kathryn, with his feet propped up on the back of a chair, Starling is still wearing his wine-colored silk bathrobe, or *dressing gown* as he likes to call it, and Luke sits between the two of them at the head of the table, straddling his chair and dressed in khakis and a light blue sweater.

But we *can* do anything we want, darling, Starling smart-aleckly replies. We're adults!

Don't you have schoolwork to do? Luke innocently asks Kathryn.

Starling laughs, a spontaneous burst, and Kathryn sticks out her tongue at Luke. Then she clears her throat and says, Well, at least *one* of us is getting an education.

I don't need a college education, Starling chimes in proudly, I'm going to be an actor.

Laughs all around.

Then he continues: Just what are you planning to do with all this education is what I want to know.

Oh, I don't know, Kathryn says, sipping her coffee. Become a writer maybe, or… (she looks at both of them over the top of her cup, mischievously) …or marry one. She finishes her sentence in a flurry, staring them down.

Luke clasps his hands behind his head playfully. Anyone particular in mind? Professor Van Doren perhaps?

Kathryn laughs and blushes at the same time. I'm just teasing, she says. Actually, I don't think I want to get married for a very long time, and certainly not before the age of thirty. Then she pauses, to give what she is about to say its fullest dramatic weight: If at all. Which is not to say that I don't want a boyfriend.

Looking out the window, Starling suddenly announces that the morning is almost half over, time is passing, there is so much to do, and they *must* seize the day! And so after yet further conversation, the threesome decide to *spend* it—like so much cash, or at least what is left of it—at the Cloisters in Tyron Park.

"Take the 8th Avenue Independent to 190th Street," Starling reads from the WPA Guide to New York City (their *bible*, they call it), as the trio emerges onto Amsterdam Avenue. And just then, suddenly, something *whooshes* Kathryn back in time. Maybe it has to do with the quality of the light, or with how the three of them are standing, each in relation to the other; she can't be quite sure just what it is exactly: but for a moment, there they are again, standing in the middle of Elm Street, ages five and six, Laird's rusting red wagon between them, and mud slipping through Starling's hands like the sand in an hourglass. Some fifteen years later, now, Kathryn's awareness of the passing of time is bittersweet. She smiles a private, unseen smile, as Starling continues to read from the Guide.

"A set of six hand-woven, fifteenth-century tapestries depicting the *Hunt of the Unicorn* was donated by Mr. Rockefeller in 1935."

Mr. Rockefeller! Kathryn and Luke *ooh* and *aah*.

"These textiles portray an allegory of the Incarnation, with Christ represented by the fabulous unicorn, symbol of purity."

The fabulous unicorn! Luke repeats the phrase.

I *am* the unicorn, Starling says, raising his wine-filled paper cup as the three of them sit in Central Park later that same afternoon. They have quickly assembled a picnic—bread, cheese, fruit, and wine—and spread themselves out on a patch of lush grass: *Déjeuner sur l'herbe*.

I've just remembered that when I was first learning how to write my name, I would also always draw pictures to accompany it, Starling says, then takes a sip of wine. I'd write the letters 'S' and 'T', and they would seem so opposite to me, like Ermine and how I thought of my father—that soft, *suss*-ing 'S', and the hard *tuh* sound of the 'T'. Then, for whatever reason, I would picture, and draw a horse with a horn coming out of the middle of its head—because that was what the letters 'S' and 'T' together, that *ST* sound, made me think of. I don't think I'd even heard of unicorns at that point, but I must have seen an illustration of one, and it just seeped into my subconscious.

I don't remember seeing those pictures, Luke says, picking grapes from the bunch, then plopping several into his mouth.

I only made them when I was alone, Starling says puckishly, and I didn't show them to anyone—not even to Ermine.

And so the conversation meanders, winding its way through the events of the day—a dash of the present moment, a dabbing of the past, and more than a touch of the future, all colored by the effects of the wine...until Kathryn says, looking up and out, as if suddenly snapped out of a trance, This is one of my favorite kinds of views—

grass, pond, trees—against a backdrop of all these great big beautiful man-made buildings; and then behind all of that—a forever of sky! She sighs and takes another sip of wine. I still can't quite believe that we've done it—that we're actually here, living here, you know?

I can believe it, Luke responds, looking intensely at his friends. I mean, we had to; we had no choice—we had to get out of there, just as much as we had to come here.

I know, Kathryn says, but weren't you scared? Come on, admit it. She looks at both of them. I know I was. And did you really think that we'd do it, that we could do it, I mean in the sense of actually being able to pull it off?

Yes, I did. Luke has suddenly become very serious, almost grim-faced. And then when the Bomb was dropped last summer, and the second one a few days after that, I just figured it was time to go somewhere, to do something, and that we might as well come here and do this, might as well follow our dreams, as much as anything else—because it seemed like we could be dead tomorrow: nothing made sense anymore, and anything seemed possible. The world had effectively been turned upside-down.

Kathryn looks up at the Empire State Building in the distance and suddenly remembers that a plane had crashed into it a couple of years earlier. She shudders. You know, that reminds me—I just read an article in that magazine *Politics*, by somebody MacDonald I think his name was; this was at work. He comes out against the Bomb, which I thought was brave, since it's not exactly a popular stance.

Gandhi spoke out against it, too, Luke says. So did Camus. Not that anybody was paying attention.

And then they go quiet, as all three seem to be reflecting on the events of the previous summer. As they sit, neither talking nor even sipping their wine, their heads almost bowed, Starling begins breaking off pieces of bread and feeding it to the many birds that have gathered.

[3]

Another Saturday morning in Manhattan, Kathryn says as she stretches.

Starling, who has dark circles under his eyes, holds his head with both hands, looks up but does not speak. Instead, he yawns repeatedly.

Somebody was out late last night, Luke mutters from behind his newspaper.

Starling does not respond.

Sensing trouble, Kathryn tries to change the subject by focusing on Luke's paper: Isn't that Lauren Bacall on the front page of the *Times*?

Starling perks up and peers at the newspaper. I just loved her in *To Have and Have Not*, he sighs.

This is serious business, Starling, Luke says, clearly irritated. She and Humphrey Bogart and several others from Hollywood have gone to Washington to protest the arrest of the Hollywood Ten. He pauses and looks around the room. The House Committee on Un-American Activities! Can you imagine? What's *Un-American*? And who defines it? I'm sure there are things all three of us have done that somebody could classify as 'Un-American'.

Kathryn shivers: It *is* frightening.

Luke glares at Starling: You might very well have been doing Un-American things just last night when you were out so late. He pauses, then adds—or should I say this morning?

Starling yawns and examines his fingernails, feigning disinterest. So?

So, I feel like we never see you anymore.

Do you miss me? Starling asks coquettishly, batting his eyelashes.

Yes, we do, Kathryn says.

Starling is finally waking up. I'm sorry, he says now, looking at his friends intently. I miss you both, too, I really do. It's just that…I'm just…so…*frustrated*. He scratches his head. It's this so-called career of mine.

What does that have to do with staying out half the night? Luke asks.

Well, *Ermine*, Starling smirks, I have to do *something* with my frustration. He looks at Luke and smiles. Why, are you jealous?

Luke's face reddens. Of what?

Kathryn breaks in: What *about* your career?

That's just it, isn't it? Starling looks at Kathryn. What *about* my career? What career? I don't have one. You know the story: we've been here for a year now and all I've gotten is one walk-on part with no lines in a television play. Nobody even knows I exist!

We know it, Starling, Kathryn says.

He cocks his head. Thank you, darling. But you know me—that's not enough. He stares off into space. There is something that I've been thinking about a lot lately, wondering—oh God, I'm almost afraid to say it out loud.

Go ahead and say it, Kathryn encourages him. Maybe we can help.

Luke nudges Starling gently with his arm.

Starling looks at his friends sadly. I've just been wondering, and starting to question, if maybe the color of my skin has something to do with my not getting parts. I guess I just thought that things would be different in New York City.

It could be, Luke says solemnly.

Kathryn shakes her head: I can't believe that; I just can't imagine it—not in Manhattan. Have you spoken with Barry about it?

Starling shakes his head 'no'.

Talk about something being Un-American! Luke says, incredulous.

I know, I know, Starling says. But the more I think about it.... Well, look—there's Lena Horne, right; she's light-skinned, like me. But she's a beautiful woman, and she sings, too. Almost all of the other colored people you see in the movies, on television, or even on Broadway, are really dark-skinned—Ethel Waters, Louis Armstrong, Hattie McDaniel...and look at the roles they all play! He pauses, thinking. Pure singers seem to do just fine. Now he smiles, remembering: There's this great story about Billie Holiday storming off the set of the movie *St. Louis* because they had her playing a maid. Can you imagine? He laughs. If anyone was less likely to play a maid!

Kathryn and Luke both smile and nod their heads in agreement.

But maybe the reason singers seem to do okay, he continues, is because way out there in *nowheresville*, places like our hometown, you don't tend to *see* them so much as you do just *hear* them on the radio and on records; and as long as they can be heard and not seen, that somehow makes it okay.

I would really hate to think that that is true, Kathryn says.

But what else could it be? Starling jumps in. It's not like most of the parts I've been trying out for require a lot of talent; I really don't think it's that.

You just need a lucky break, that's all, Luke says.

Yeah, *that's all*, Starling responds sarcastically. And how do you suppose I get that?

I think you should talk to Barry about all of this, Kathryn says, and see what he has to say; he might have some prior experience, maybe with another client....

Barry, Luke exclaims. It's such a perfect name for an agent.

Starling hangs his head: I just thought it would all be easier.

Luke reaches across the table, grabs Starling's hand and squeezes it, then lets go.

Kathryn stands now and rubs Starling's head momentarily, then leaves the room.

Starling starts to sob openly, shuddering, and Luke moves next to him and puts an arm around his shoulder. Starling nudges his way into Luke's embrace, resting his head on Luke's shoulder.

Kathryn calls from the other room that she has forgotten something at the office and is going to retrieve it.

Luke squeezes Starling's shoulder with his strong hand, and then says, Do you want to talk about it?

Starling seems startled by the question, wipes his eyes and asks, About what?

Luke shrugs. Everything, I guess. Anything. Last night. All the other nights. You. Me....

I still love you, if that's what you mean, Starling says, sniffling.

Don't, Luke winces.

And what I do at night is just my way of dealing with it.

I worry about you.

Sometimes I wonder if this is really the best thing, Starling says, tentatively but with a slightly cruel edge to his voice. You know—our living together. I find myself wondering if maybe it wouldn't be easier for me if we didn't live in the same apartment.

Luke just looks at him, his face as blank as a poker chip, and says coldly: Kathryn would be devastated if you moved out.

And you? Starling asks.

Now Luke is irritated again. Oh come on, Star, I would miss you, too, of course I would; you know that. But we've had this conversation: I love you, but I am not *in love* with you.

Yeah? Starling is getting angry now. Well, if you're not a fairy, then why aren't you dating women?

I...I don't know; I just don't feel ready, Luke says calmly and deliberately. I need time to sort everything out.

What's 'everything'?

Luke steels himself. My feelings....

About what?

About *everything*: about my brother and how much I still miss him and think that I may never get over losing him, and about my parents and how they treated me and Laura, about you and Kathryn, and just about myself and life in general. I need time to think. He looks at Starling now, as he is about to turn the tables. You know about time, don't you?—I think you've got way too much of it on your hands.

And what do you suggest I do?

I don't know, but why don't you make it something constructive for a change, instead of destructive, or should I say self-destructive? Maybe you should get a part-time job, something that would allow you to continue to go on auditions. And then with the money from a part-time job you could afford to take acting lessons.

Which you obviously think I need.

That is not what I said, Starling. But it is one way to test this question you have about prejudice: take acting lessons and become so good at your craft that producers and directors can't *not* hire you, and then if they don't, you'll know why, you'll have your answer.

You don't know what I do with my time, Starling says defiantly. And besides, you changed the subject.

Now *you've* changed the subject, Luke laughs. What is the subject, anyway?

The subject was you and your need to think about everything.

So?

Starling shrugs. So, I don't know—how long do you think you'll need?

There's no way I can quantify it, Star—how can I say that it will take me such and such a period of time to figure everything out? I can't; I don't even know for sure what 'everything' is, or just what I have to figure out. Hell, I may never figure it all out.

Oh, great! Starling hits his forehead with the palm of his hand. And meanwhile, I'm supposed to do...what?

What do you mean, meanwhile you're supposed to do what? One thing has nothing to do with the other: just get on with your life, that's all.

Starling stands up suddenly; the metal chair leg scrapes against the floor. Just get on with my life, huh? Well, that's what staying out late has been about—just trying to get on with my life. But that's obviously not good enough for you. He leaves the room and calls back as he goes: I'm moving out. And then the door slams.

[4]

I t is May, leafy May in the artificial lights of Manhattan, when evenings are just beginning to lengthen after the long winter. The threesome has come up to Harlem for the evening, to the famed Apollo Theatre on 125th Street. Kathryn and Luke are still living in the same apartment on West 110th Street, but Starling has, indeed, moved out, which for a while caused a rupture of their threesome. But within the past year they have had a reconciliation, and now they usually see each other several times a week. Kathryn has finished college but for the time being has decided against going on to graduate school and is working full-time in the English Department at Barnard. Luke has moved up in his profession and is now an editorial assistant at Farrar, Straus in Union Square. And Starling is living in the Village with a man over twenty-five years his senior. Neither Kathryn nor Luke like Anton, a moody, possessive Russian émigré, though they tried in the beginning, and by now there is an unspoken agreement with Starling that whenever the three of them get together, Anton will not be with him. Starling still goes on the occasional audition, but with neither the frequency nor the fervency that he did that first year in Manhattan. He is not working, nor is he hungry; he is essentially being kept.

But tonight they have come up to Harlem, to the Apollo, to hear the now legendary Billie Holiday, whose records they, particularly Starling, have been collecting for years. Because of Holiday's drug arrest, her cabaret card has been taken away and she can no longer perform at any venue in the state of New York where alcohol is served. Thus in New York, at least, she must play these larger concert halls, which are less appropriate to her intimate style.

The atmosphere inside the packed theatre is charged and electric, yet it is also hushed, perhaps from the knowledge that someone great is just backstage, just behind that door, behind that drapery or down that hallway. The audience is a mix of black and white; Kathryn, Luke, and Starling sit near the front, center stage (Starling is in the middle). Though the theatre seats over fifteen hundred, an attempt has been made, especially with the lighting, to give the place the intimacy of a small club, and it has been largely successful.

I still can't believe that we're finally going to see her in person, Kathryn says. Starling rolls his eyes and smiles: Don't be so déclassé, darling, it's just Lady Day; be sophisticated.

Actually, Kathryn says, musing, I wouldn't be surprised if she appreciates a certain reverence, if not demands it.

Me too, Starling says, I was just teasing. He pauses, then adds: And I think she deserves it, too.

After all, Kathryn says, she didn't get the name 'Lady Day' for nothing—she earned it.

Suddenly, the big room goes dark. Kathryn grabs Starling's hand. There is brief applause, and then so much whispering that, collectively, it causes a din in the room. Someone shushes the crowd loudly, more than once, and the room goes silent.

There is a hoarse cough, a smoker's cough. It is recognizably *her* voice, *her* cough—she is somewhere in the house, though she still cannot be seen. Slowly, a small spot of light appears on the fine maple floor of the stage, a floor revered by dancers; it is a pin light, and it gradually widens and becomes a circle of light, a whole beaming moon of light which engulfs her and only her. And then there she is—Miss Billie Holiday. The applause is thunderous, deafening.

She is dressed in a slinky, shimmering gold dress with matching gloves to the elbow, and she is much thinner than she has appeared in recent years. As if to emphasize this new, sleek elegance, her hair is severely pulled back from her face into a ponytail, and there is a cluster of what appear to be diamonds in her ears. She is leaning against a stool and looking down at the floor. Behind her, one can see just the slightest glimmer of the other players, and especially the glinting of their instruments—piano, bass, drums, and saxophone, though slowly, gradually, the spotlight widens to include them. Now she looks up, out, and over the heads of the audience, to some seemingly fixed horizon line. She is a fiercely handsome woman, if also ravaged: her vices are legendary. She approaches the microphone as if it were a lover, then opens her mouth to sing and the spotlight seems to flood into it, dredging up all that darkness, catching on her white teeth, sparkling, dazzling, just as she intones the first words of the first song: "April in Paris".

Kathryn, Luke, and Starling are rapt, as is the entire audience. *This* is drama. Starling notices how Holiday holds herself: there is a certain abandon in her body, as if she is not inhabiting it, has somehow left it, and he pays close attention, too, to how Lady Day moves, which is not much at all. She seems, he thinks, to be keeping time to the music subtly, with her head and with her mouth (between notes), the way a lot of bass players do; there is only an occasional movement of the hand or the arm, usually originating from the elbow or the shoulder—a little *swing* of movement, or a slight sawing motion. And of course, there is also what she is now famous for, her trademark (or one of them, for there are no gardenias in her hair tonight)—she is singing, and moving, just ever so slightly *behind the beat*. Starling has felt such a kinship with Holiday for so long that he believes he can learn from her, and so he is, in fact, studying her, with all of the eagerness and avidity of a student.

There is warm applause when she finishes "April in Paris". Holiday thanks the audience politely but she does not chat; instead, she turns around and briefly talks to the members of her band, then slowly faces the crowd again and launches into the next song, "A Foggy Day in London Town". She sings for an hour and a half—"Autumn in New York", "Blue Moon", "What a Little Moonlight Can Do", "Moonlight in Vermont", "Lover Man", "Fine and Mellow", "Don't Explain", and on and on—closing with "God Bless the Child". And then as an encore, in a cold, blue spotlight, she performs "Strange Fruit", by now her signature number: the audience has been waiting for it.

> Here is a fruit for the crows to pluck,
> For the rain to gather, for the wind to suck,
> For the sun to rot, for a tree to drop,
> Here is a strange and bitter crop.

And just after she sings the last word of the song, *crop*, a word that she cries, that she creates an arc with, because it holds a life—the room is swept in darkness once again, and that darkness is held, possibly for as long as a minute. Then the house lights are gradually raised, and she is gone.

Kathryn and Luke both look over to see that Starling is in tears, and now there is thunderous applause and foot-stomping and whistling, too, but Lady Day does not, and will not, come back.

Standing along with most everyone else in the theatre, Starling puts one hand dramatically over his heart, then throws out his hands to indicate that there are no words, that he is speechless.

Kathryn also stands and puts an arm around Starling. You're right—the woman is an artist.

Luke joins the two, standing.

Starling looks at Kathryn and Luke and takes their hands: I'll remember this evening forever. I love you both.

Kathryn squeezes his hand. We love you too, Starling.

Starling beams: I can die happy now—you both love me *and* we've seen Billie Holiday.

[5]

Luke is walking about the city on a Saturday morning alone and thinking about a book he has recently read in galleys, *A Walker in the City*; it is a title he especially likes. Strolling up the Avenue of the Americas, having just crossed 59th, he is heading Downtown—for no particular reason other than that it is where his feet and his nose seem to be taking him today. It is a crisp, beautiful June day, the sky is cloudless and brightly blue, and yet he feels lost: weekends have become difficult since Starling moved out, and now that Kathryn is seeing someone regularly and frequently not at home, he doesn't know quite what to do with himself on these weekends when he is alone in the apartment, and there are moments when he feels frightened, realizing just how far away from home he is, and knowing, too, that there is no going back. *You Can't Go Home Again.*

But where to turn? What to do?

He leaves the apartment and walks (at least he gets out, is a walker in the city, he tells himself)—sometimes from mid-morning until late afternoon, or even into the early evening. And then he returns home, eats dinner if he hasn't eaten out, reads, and falls asleep. Then comes Sunday, another day....

It will be all right, he tells himself now as he crosses 54th; he just hasn't found a rhythm to these days yet.

He knows it's ludicrous—he is in Manhattan for Christ sakes! There is *so much* to do here. He successfully avoided having to serve in the army, he reminds himself—escaped possibly being sent to Korea: he should be thrilled. He crosses over to Fifth and continues walking Downtown.

Just be brave, he tells himself. He has been brave in the past. He stood up to his father, who *always* terrified him. He defended Starling. He is less sure, however, about having survived Laird's death. Yes, he, Luke, is alive, but.... He thinks of lions now, symbols of bravery, and then he pictures the majestic stone beasts that guard the entrance to the New York Public Library. He is only blocks away.

He knows the area well. The *New York Times* building is close by. So are the offices of *The New Yorker*. Now he can relax somewhat, let his mind go, let it unreel. Immediately, it takes him back to when he was on his own, living at the boarding house and working in the library; Kathryn was away at school, and he and Starling weren't speaking. He was fine then; he even enjoyed some of it. He was resourceful; he was brave. He can do that, *be* that, again, he tells himself. Only now his opponent is less specific. Now his enemy is time itself. But all he really needs to get through the weekends less painfully, he realizes, is structure—structure and meaning.

And then suddenly, there are the lions, the library. He stops at the foot of the one closest to him, rests his hand on its paw, and then gazes out in the same direction that the lion is looking, as if he is inhabiting it.

I am a lion, he tells himself. And then he remembers, several years back—hadn't Starling compared himself to a unicorn? *The lion and the unicorn*—Orwell's title. But this is no good: thinking about Starling is weakening him, because he misses Starling, he can admit that here and now; and yet he also knows from experience that Starling can't be depended upon.

He, Luke, must be self-reliant. A self-reliant, roaring, lion!

He runs the palm of his hand over the smooth stone now as people pass by, on their way up and down the steps, into and out of the building.

He needs to get back to swimming, he tells himself—he had swam every day back home when he was living at the boarding house; that will help. He knows there is a YMCA not too far from the office, at 23rd and 6th. He could swim early on Saturday and Sunday mornings, breakfast out, and then go into the office for a while—there is always so much work to be done; he never finishes it all during the week.

I am a lion, he thinks. *A young lion,* but a lion nevertheless.

[6]

An August evening, and Starling has moved back into the old apartment with Kathryn and Luke. He is once again regularly making the rounds, and he has gotten the occasional small part, too—mostly on television; still nothing on Broadway, and his longest line thus far is a mere sentence. To pay the rent he has taken a part-time job as a waiter in a neighborhood restaurant. Meanwhile, Kathryn, with Luke's help, has joined him at Farrar, Straus, working as a first reader.

A weekday evening, just after dinner, and the three are sitting in the living room; it is a hot summer night and the windows are wide open, so there is traffic and street noise coming into the room. Luke and Starling both have bottles of beer at their feet and are reading the *New York Times*. Kathryn is drinking lemonade and appears to be engrossed in a paperback book.

Luke looks over at Kathryn: Are you still reading Ayn Rand?

Kathryn smirks and responds, Adroitly.

The sensation! Luke says, rolling his eyes.

So they say, Kathryn says. But truth be told, I find her rather bad.

Luke smiles: So I've heard. You know she testified before HUAC, don't you? She actually identified as Communist propaganda the fact that the Russians in some American film were depicted as smiling.

Kathryn's jaw drops.

It's true, Luke says. It's a matter of public record; you can look it up.

She laughs ruefully and shakes her head: I'd rather be reading Mary McCarthy any day.

Now *there's* an interesting woman.

Yes, I just adored *The Company She Keeps*, Kathryn says intently. Wouldn't you love to meet her?

Luke nods and mumbles, Mmm.

She often writes for *Politics*, you know?

He nods again.

Starling lowers the newspaper and joins in: But I don't understand why you're reading Miss Rand when you'd rather be reading Miss McCarthy?

Curiosity—I just wanted to see what all the fuss was about. Kathryn laughs: And now I feel compelled to finish the damn thing.

So is the cat dead? Luke asks, chuckling.

I'll say, Kathryn replies with a laugh.

Starling is clearly enjoying this domestic scene. Lazily, lovingly, he asks Luke what he is reading.

Luke ruffles the newspaper: The paper, silly, same as you.

Starling shakes his head: What I mean is, what are you reading *about*? For example (as if he were talking to a child) I am reading about a new play that's coming to Broadway; it will star Julie Harris and is called *I Am a Camera*; remember how fabulous she was in *A Member of the Wedding*? He looks down at the newspaper. It's based on a book of stories by Christopher Isherwood, set in Berlin.

Berlin Stories, Luke says knowingly.

Kathryn stretches: Berlin. Paris. London…when *are* we going to Europe anyway?

I'm reading about Julius Rosenberg, Luke says, responding to Starling's question, the guy who's been arrested for giving secrets to the Russians.

Starling provocatively raises one eyebrow and lowers his voice: What kind of secrets?

Luke is distracted, still reading: About the Bomb.

Starling groans and takes a swig from his beer: I'd much rather read about Julie Harris any day.

Kathryn clears her throat dramatically: Ahem! I said, when *are* we going to Europe?

Luke laughs as he peers over the top of the paper: Probably when we can afford to. And, he adds, returning to the paper, his voice trailing off, when I can afford to take the time away from work.

Starling looks at Kathryn now: Didn't you say you had a date tonight, darling?

Kathryn narrows her eyes: Are you trying to get rid of me?

Is this with the mystery man again? Luke asks.

She stands and sighs, then looks at the clock: I suppose I should start getting myself ready.

And what shall we do with our fine selves this evening? Starling asks Luke.

Oh, I don't know, Luke shrugs, thinking. Do you want to go down to the Village, maybe have a drink at the San Remo, something like that?

Sure, Starling says enthusiastically. Or would you rather go to Marie's Crisis Café, or the White Horse, or the Limelight, or just over to the West End?

Luke sits up straight and puts down the newspaper: Let's hop the train downtown and decide when we get there; I'd rather not go to the West End tonight.

And so the two make their way downtown to the Village, emerging at Sheridan Square and then walking down to MacDougal

Street and the San Remo. The bar is crowded and noisy, as usual, but Luke and Starling manage to find the one remaining table, sit down and order; both continue to drink beer from the bottle.

What do you think about the idea of you, me, and Kathryn trying to find an apartment in the Village? Starling asks Luke now.

Actually, Luke says, Kathryn and I were just starting to talk about that right before you came back. Now that we're both working in Union Square, I think we should do it.

Starling swigs his beer: Mmm. The only thing is—I wonder if I would always be afraid of running into Anton (he looks around the room). God, I hope we don't see him tonight; I hadn't even thought of it, or rather, of him.

Luke makes a face: I hope not, too, Star, but New York's a big place, you know?

Starling looks at Luke contritely: Do you think you could ever forgive me for that?

There's nothing to forgive, Luke says dismissively.

Starling shakes his head: I don't know what I was thinking. Then he laughs: I guess that's just it—I wasn't thinking.

Luke places a hand on Starling's shoulder: Well, don't give it another thought.

Starling smiles warmly and says, Thanks, Luke, then takes a swig of beer and looks around. But I'll tell you what I would like to give another thought to, and that's this mystery man that Kathryn's been seeing: aren't you curious?

Of course I'm curious.

Any guesses who it is? Starling asks mischievously. We don't even have a first name to go on.

Luke smiles, lifts the beer bottle to his lips to drink, then lowers it: My guess is that it's somebody from Columbia. Maybe a professor.

That must be right! Starling says, I hadn't made the connection, but she did start seeing Mr. X a couple of months ago, didn't she, just before she left the job there?

Luke nods: Yep.

What if she marries him? Starling asks thoughtfully, and moves out on us?

Luke laughs: Hey, wait a minute! Don't you think you're rushing things a bit?

I know, but what if she does?

Luke looks away momentarily, distracted by something across the room: Kathryn's not the type to rush into things.

I'm not saying that she would, Starling says. But what if, a year or two down the road, she marries him and moves out, and then it's just the two of us living in the apartment?

Starling seems to be trying to get at something here, something that is clearly just beginning to make Luke feel uncomfortable, but before the conversation can go any further, they are interrupted. A fight has broken out on the other side of the room, with several people yelling and the sound of chairs scraping against the floor.

Luke and Starling look over to see a group of five or six young men, all obviously drunk, standing around a table, shouting at and threatening its occupants. It appears that the fight has to do with a Negro man being with two white women. The words *Nigger* and *Queer* are hurled, and then fists and chairs begin to fly, until an all-out brawl ensues. Stunned, caught up in observing the scene, and unsure of what they should do, before Luke and Starling are even aware of it, two other young men, apparently from the same group, are standing at *their* table and looking down at them, their faces red and scowling:

And what're you two queers doing here? one of them says.

Luke stands up to defend Starling and himself, but because he is in between sitting and standing, his knees bent, and because he has already had a few beers, even though he is bigger than both of these young men, a single swing from one of them takes him down, and he falls to the floor. And now the two turn to Starling and begin pummeling him with their fists and hurling the same epithets that they had at the Negro at the other table—*Nigger! Queer!*

Before long, both Luke and Starling have disappeared from view as the fighting grows and the crowd gathers around.

[7]

June 1953, and Kathryn has moved out, eloping—about a year and a half ago—with the mystery man she had been dating, a famous poet twelve years her senior, thus marrying, at twenty-seven, well before the age of thirty—yet still late for a woman of her time and place. The poet, Richard Lincoln, hails from a wealthy New England family that owns several properties in Manhattan, one of which is a fashionable townhouse on Central Park West, where he and Kathryn now live.

Luke and Starling are still living in the same Greenwich Village apartment they shared briefly with Kathryn on Carmine Street. It is smaller than their previous digs on West 110th, more a cluster of cubicles than a long and narrow railroad car, but it also has much more charm than the other place—a set of French doors, a fireplace, gumwood trim, etcetera.

Kathryn's marriage has not been easy: though she adores Richard, and the two have much in common, he suffers from some as-yet-undiagnosed mental illness, and there have been terrible, harrowing scenes. Most of the time he is lucid and fine and their connection is deep, their conversations stimulating, but at other times he is a raving lunatic, and there is just no predicting when he will go off, which makes social functions particularly tense for Kathryn, who has taken up smoking.

Thus, she is not at all happy about and did not want to host, much less attend the dinner party at which she now finds herself, and to which Luke and Starling were decidedly not invited. But Richard had said that Mr. So-and-So, an internationally renowned novelist/painter/sculptor/composer/poet/you-name-it, was visiting (it was usually from some eastern European country, say—Macedonia), and that he must, as an American poet of his stature, play host, which meant that Kathryn must play hostess.

The dining room is an elegant affair, with floor-to-ceiling windows overlooking Central Park, covered by a sheer dove-gray drapery, which billows in and out of the room, like so much smoke. A long, rectangular table, perfectly placed and set for ten, dominates the room, and in the center of the table there is a baroque silver candelabrum, the centerpiece, that holds ten lit candles. All in all, it looks like the set of a thirties Hollywood movie.

Dressed in a simple sleeveless long white evening dress, Kathryn opens the French doors that lead into the dining room, and the guests slowly file in. This is not the bohemian set—no, these people are dressed to the nines: There is Mr. So-and-So, the internationally renowned novelist/painter/sculptor/composer/poet/you-name-it, and his petite wife, followed by two other renowned (if not necessarily respected) American writers (writers A and B), trailed by their wives and/or mistresses (Kathryn can't keep track of which—nor is it easily discernable, since both are dressed like prostitutes), and lastly, there is also a man representing the U.S. government, perhaps a diplomat to Mr. So-and So's country, and *his* wife. Among Kathryn's multitude of feelings on this occasion are anger and resentfulness that Luke and Starling were not invited, and thus there is no one there *for her*.

Before dinner, the men and women have been separated, as

usual, and the moment Kathryn first sees her husband in the dining room, she immediately notices that he has the distracted look that often precedes one of his attacks. She will watch him like a hawk, she thinks, and she will not be able to eat. She has been seated next to the wives/mistresses of writers A and B, neither of whom she has met before.

The wife/mistress of Writer B now asks her and the wife/mistress of Writer A if either of them has read the book by that Negro boy everyone is talking about; something with 'mountain' in the title?

The wife/mistress of Writer A immediately puts down her fork and exclaims, Oh, you must mean *Go Tell It on the Mountain*? No, I haven't read it yet, and I doubt that I will.

Well, says the wife/mistress of Writer B, I always try to make a point of reading the bestsellers as soon as I possibly can. She takes a sip of her wine.

They both probably like Ayn Rand, Kathryn thinks, trying to decide whether or not she should speak her mind. She lights a cigarette and drinks from her wine glass so as to stall for time; then she eyes her husband, who appears to be fine, seemingly engaged in a normal conversation at the opposite end of the table. And so she decides to throw caution to the wind. What the hell!

First of all, his name is James Baldwin, she says, and he's not a boy, he's a man. She scratches one hand with the other, a recently developed nervous tic. And secondly, *Go Tell It on the Mountain* is more than just a bestseller; it's a work of literature.

With this, Kathryn's end of the table goes completely silent, while at the other end of the table, Mr. So-and-So, who has heard only Kathryn's last word, 'literature', pounces.

Literature, literature—why must we always at these dinner parties speak of literature, eh? Especially when there are far more important matters to be discussed. He looks at his wife: Am I not right, my little one?

She nods and coos but does not speak.

And besides, he continues, *orating* now, and clearly enjoying the sound of his own voice: What is there to be said about literature, really? We must write it instead, eh? He looks at Lincoln for his response.

Well, yes, of course, Richard says gingerly, we must write it, he laughs, pushing a strand of graying hair behind his ear. Slowly now, emphasizing every word, he repeats the phrase: We...must...write...it. But it is not so surprising that we should also like to talk about it, is it? After all, it is our *schlock* in trade.

From the opposite end of the table, Kathryn is now scrutinizing her husband, worried that he is about to break.

Perhaps what you are saying, the diplomat says, looking at Mr. So-and-So, if I may suggest this, is that in my country there is not enough emphasis on or knowledge of politics, public affairs, and history.

Mr. So-and-So waves his hand dismissively: Well, yes, of course, everyone knows that is true of Americans, eh? It is such common knowledge, so universally understood, in fact, that it need not even be stated. No, what I am talking about, and *all* that I am talking about, is simple conversation, dinner table 'chat', I believe you Americans call it.

Richard says now, Might I suggest that if you don't like this conversation, you go to the other end of the table.

This is Kathryn's chance, her cue to step in as she has done so many times before, to embrace the entire room, to save the day. But because of the inherent hostility in her husband's suggestion, and also because she is worn down, she simply cannot muster the energy.

The diplomat leans into the conversation now, attempting to shield Mr. So-and-So from Richard. He sends a look of alarm down the table to Kathryn, then clears his throat and laughs: I think what our fine host really means, he says, glancing at Mr. So-and-So, is— what would *you* like to talk about this evening, what sort of conversation do you feel would be worthy of your visit? He looks around the table for help, smiling tightly. Because I am certain that all of us here at this table want you to take something valuable and worthwhile home with you from your visit to America. He pauses, and once again smiles forcefully. Along with fond memories, of course.

Mr. So-and-So nods: Well, let us then talk about those two poor people who were just murdered, those martyrs, eh? Mr. and Mrs. Rosenberg. He looks round the table. We, my wife and I, along with our fellow countrymen, we cannot believe what your country has done to those two people, he says, raising his voice now. It is barbaric! Execution! Electric chair! We have no such thing in my country, nor in all of Europe. It is positively barbaric. You call yourselves a civilized nation, eh? And then you murder these two people—citizens, a mother and a father with two small children, young boys now orphaned. You murder them, and for what? For having different beliefs from your own, eh? Is that a crime? It is barbaric, I tell you, for a government to murder its own citizens—it is no less than what a savage or an animal would do.

He leans back from the table, satisfied, but then obviously remembers something, laughs, and says, And now your fine United States of America has banned Charlie Chaplin from re-entering the country. Charlie Chaplin—the little tramp! He laughs uproariously. It's absurd!

Kathryn sits tensely at the other end of the table, smoking, watching her husband and wondering what, if anything, she should do; and wondering, too, if the evening could possible get any worse, when in fact it does.

Richard is picking up peas, one at a time, and slowly placing them on the tines of his fork, which he has balanced over the edge of his plate. I think you're a Communist, is what I think, he finally says, peering up from his peas. A Pinko. A Red. Now he hits the end of the fork so that the peas boomerang into the face of Mr. So-and So, and then he begins violently stabbing at his empty plate with it, successfully cracking the china in two.

He stands suddenly, pushing back his chair with such force that it falls over: You and your type are all over the country now. But you have no business, no business but show business, which is to say monkey business, being in the U. S. of A., much less in this room and at this table, you and your little mouse of a wife there. Isn't that right, Kathryn?

Looking down the table at his wife, he does not wait for her response. He turns back to Mr. So-and-So and points to the door, screaming now: SO JUST GET UP AND GET OUT—NOW! He pauses and looks at his adversary's wife, then adds: BOTH O' YA'S!!

Kathryn immediately punches out her cigarette, stands up from the table and, in a quivering voice, apologizes to her guests and asks everyone to leave as quickly as possible. She catches the eye of the diplomat who, as if on command, suddenly assumes the role of usher; then she goes over to her husband, eases him down into his chair and places her hands firmly on his shoulders. Once the room has cleared, she lays her head on his shoulder and slides her hands down his torso, holding him tightly; and, as always in these difficult moments, she closes her eyes and tries to remember the very moment she and Richard first met (in the auditorium after his reading, Van Doren introduced them), when it had seemed, almost immediately, as if their marriage was meant to be, fated.

[8]

1956

Kathryn, Luke, and Starling are now all three in their
early thirties, certainly sadder than they were at the age of five and
six when they first met, if not also (in all cases) wiser. Kathryn and
Richard have moved to Boston, where he is teaching at Harvard, but
also so that he can be closer to his doctor at Massachusetts General
Hospital. As might have been expected, Starling has moved out once
again and is living by himself in a studio apartment in Spanish Harlem. Only Luke has remained stationary—he is still working as an
editor at Farrar, Straus, and he is also still occupying the same apartment on Carmine Street in the Village that the three once shared; in
fact, he has recently bought it. The threesome last saw each other in
August, shortly before Kathryn and Richard moved away; now that

Kathryn is gone, Luke and Starling see one another rarely, *Only once in a very pink moon*, as Starling puts it.

Starling's existence has become, over time, increasingly depressed and depraved: he rarely bothers to go on auditions anymore, and he has had a difficult time holding onto any of a variety of jobs for very long, and so there have been a debilitating and demoralizing succession of them. Now all he does is stay out late partying most nights, drinking and smoking marijuana, and he has also just recently begun trading sex for money—not that he is walking the streets, but rather it is simply known, in certain circles of the neighborhood, that this still pretty if beginning to fade and now rougher-around-the-edges mulatto boy, is, as they say, *willing*; in short, he has developed something of a reputation, and a clientele.

Starling's apartment is a shambles—cluttered, disorderly, and also dirty; it consists of one living/bed-room, a small kitchenette, and a bathroom. Opposite the front door is the bed, a twin bed that is unmade; the floor is littered with trash, plates and wrappers of half-eaten food, shoes, clothing, empty liquor bottles, etcetera. On the wall over the bed in huge letters is a quote from Federico Garcia Lorca's *Poet in New York*: "The boys lay inert in the cross of a yawn and stretched muscle."

Wearing the same wine-colored dressing gown he has worn for years—it is now over ten years old, torn and tattered—Starling is lying in bed talking on the telephone, drinking whiskey on ice and chain smoking, one bare leg crossed over the other, nervously playing with the phone cord, twisting it endlessly, repeatedly, and constantly shaking his crossed leg.

I am just so sick and tired of everything, he is saying. His words are slurred. I need a rest, a break, you know? I guess I just need to get out of New York City for a while. But I am so sick and tired of myself, too, and how do I get a break from me? He laughs. You're sick of me, too—that's really funny! But seriously, how do you get rid of yourself—for a while? I've been trying to do that. Where do I go? He looks around the room. Where is there for me to go? I can't go home anymore—that's not an option. He sips his whiskey. I'm just so tired all the time. Tired of all the people, too—everybody; everywhere you go, there are so many people—seems like somebody's behind every corner, every door, always somebody there, everywhere! And I'm tired of it; it takes a toll on you after awhile. He pauses to light a cigarette. And I've had it with the theater, too—with that world and all of the people in it: all the fakery and the glitter and the big egos running around. He sighs. You know I came here—it was ten years ago this fall—I came here with all of my little hopes and dreams; I know— just like everybody else, right? He puffs. And where are those dreams now? They're gone. Up in smoke. He blows smoke. Gone with the wind. Torn and tattered, and...tarnished. I don't even have them anymore; I don't think I have any dreams left. It's all about survival now, just getting from one day to the next, one foot in front of the other. But surviving for what? What am I living for, waiting for? He sighs. I feel like I've been running in circles for years. Just spinning my wheels, like one of those laboratory rats. An animal in a cage, pacing back and forth: Little not-even-Black Sambo running around in circles, chased by so many tigers. It's like I'm just going through the paces, you know? But without any feeling. And I don't know how to stop it. I don't know. I guess it's just gotten me down, dragged me down, but not under—at least not yet anyway. He takes another sip from the glass. But New York just isn't what I thought it would be; I thought I'd have a thousand opportunities, you know? Instead of having doors constantly slammed in my face simply because of the color of my skin, I do a few teleplays and then they tell me I'm over-exposed, that because of my *special look*, they say, I over-expose more quickly! And it's all just so damn depressing. He puts out one cigarette and immediately lights another. Hey, that reminds me—did you read about what happened to Jimmy Baldwin recently? It was just like what happened to Luke and me that time at the San Remo. But this was James Baldwin! He wasn't at the Remo, though, he was someplace else in the Village, maybe it was The White Horse. He pauses, thinking. No, now I remember, it was reported in the newspaper; it was at the Paddock. Anyway, Baldwin's in there having a few drinks with a white man and two white women, friends of his, you know, and they're drinking and talking and having a good ol' time, but then some guys who're also there, and drunk out of their minds, white guys, of course, they spot Baldwin and his friends and go over to their table, and then they just start yelling at them—'What's a nigger doing in here with white girls?' That kind of thing. And then the next thing you know, it turns into a real fight and Baldwin gets beaten up pretty badly and has to go to the hospital. He gulps down the remainder of the whiskey in his glass. And if that's what this country does to its own, I mean, Baldwin is one of the most celebrated writers in America today. This happened in New York, man. I mean, even the Village isn't safe anymore. I guess this is what Luke was trying to tell me about McCarthy—how he's poisoned everything. The word on the street is that these troublemakers were mostly Irish guys from the surrounding areas, and that it's some kind of a territorial thing. Not that the reason really matters. He pauses to blow several smoke rings. Anyway, I heard that Baldwin went to Paris. Moved there for good. Maybe that's what I need to do, too—move to Paris. Josephine Baker did it. Or at least maybe move to somewhere in Europe. He shakes his head. I don't know. All I know is, I need something, and I need it soon. You know what I mean? I need it real fast. He snaps his fingers. Else I feel like I'm gonna jump out of my skin. He yawns and looks at the Lorca quote over his bed and recites it in a whisper: 'The boys lay inert on the cross of a yawn and stretched muscle,' he reads, then yawns again. So anyway, listen baby, what're you doin' tonight? You got any stuff or know anybody who's got any? He crushes out his cigarette. Any kinda party goin' on you happen to know about? He laughs. Maybe that's what I need, a party, yeah, another party. He laughs again. I hear ya, baby. Partied out, huh? Pooped. Yeah, I think maybe I am, too. Maybe I should just stay in tonight and be quiet. He looks around the apartment. Clean up this dump. He laughs. How many times have you heard me say that, right? I know, I know. At least a hundred, right? He laughs again. I know—who am I kidding? I'll be out there on the street in no time, looking around for something good, for something to happen, for some kind of a party—even if it's just with one other person. But hey, sometimes that's the best kind of party, you know? Just you and them and whatever happens. He lights another cigarette. For a while there I thought that maybe I'd found that other person. Someone special. No, not Luke—this was after Luke, at a time when I thought that there wasn't anyone else for me and never would be. His name was Cole. Yep, that's right, Cole, like coleslaw. He was hip baby, let me tell you. An actor. A southern boy. Sweet—a real catch. And we were happy for a time, too (under his breath)—until I scared him away. And he was half and half, like me, so I can't blame it on that. Sighs. No, I think it was just me and who I am; I'm always scaring people away, you know? He laughs. Luke? No, we hardly ever see each other anymore. Almost never. Sure I miss him. But the whole thing is just so fucked-up. He says he's not a fairy and that's that. And my response to him is, okay, fine, but I know you love me; I *know* you do—I know he does. So I don't care what you call yourself, you can call yourself Ethel Merman or Truman Capote for all I care. Just get yourself on over here. But he won't have it; he can't, for whatever reason. And so now when we do get together, which is really only once in the pinkest of pink moons, when we do get together it's just so damned uncomfortable, and I guess that's probably my fault (he sighs), because I just can't seem to let it go, to let *him* go, and so I push, which only makes him run in the opposite direction. There've been a couple of times over the years where I've seen him out on the street, he's usually with somebody—a man or a woman—and he sees me, too, I know he does, but he pretends that he doesn't. That really hurts. Like I'm invisible or something—the original Invisible Man. He sighs again, lights another cigarette. No, that's just one more dream dashed. He lets out another big sigh. Yeah, I suppose I may as well just start getting myself ready to go out, huh? Might just as well face that thing, right? Because that's what I'm gonna do anyway. That's what I'll do—eventually, whether it's as soon as I hang up the phone, or later. I'll be out there lookin' around. He scans the room again. Ain't no use staying in here, sitting around feeling sorry for myself, that's for sure, right? He laughs. I don't see no boys layin' inert, yawnin' and stretchin' their muscles in here, do you, hon? At least not yet anyway, but the night is young, he laughs again. All right, sugar, I'm gonna go now. I'm gonna go and get myself ready to go out—hit the street, make the scene, what have you. I'll talk to you another pretty evenin'. Bye-bye for now.

[9]

*S*ome *other spring*, and Luke and Starling have taken the train up to Boston together, both on their best behavior, to spend a long weekend with Kathryn at her place; it is an opportunity she said she wanted to take advantage of while Richard is away in Europe. Though it is no longer simple between the three friends, because of their long history together, that context also deepens and enriches their every meeting, where one word, or just a look, holds so much more—and all three of them know it.

Both Kathryn and Luke appear much the same, if slightly older, but Starling has undergone a dramatic transformation: he is thinner than Kathryn and Luke have ever seen him (some would say gaunt), he dresses only in black and/or white, and his hair is now almost shoulder length and always worn pulled back tightly into a small ponytail at the nape of his neck. He has also, once again, changed what he wants to be called; now his name is *Ling*, he tells his friends, adding that for some time he has been paring down his life, living and eating more simply and healthily, under the influence of the Orientals; he is also, he adds, studying Zen Buddhism. He is through with the theater, he goes on, *finished*, because it isn't healthy for him. 'All longing produces suffering,' he quotes. He has a humble and respectable job now, cleaning office buildings in the evening; it is good for him, he tells them, because it keeps him out of trouble, but more importantly because it is cleansing, physical and not mental, and also because it makes him feel as though he is giving something back to society by helping to keep it clean. Such talk sounds eerily familiar to Kathryn, reminiscent of things she's heard from Richard, and she is worried about Starling, but she says nothing.

The Japanese magnolias that adorn much of Marlborough Street are in full blossom and fragrance, and at this time of night, in shadow, they resemble nothing less than so many large, labyrinthine ears, imagery that sadly evokes the trademark flower behind the ear of Billie Holiday, whom they have just returned from seeing at Boston's famed Storyville jazz club. Though Starling says that he no longer drinks or goes to clubs, he found the opportunity to see Lady Day one more time irresistible (just as he still, at times, finds other temptations beyond his power to resist). But the Billie Holiday that Starling, Luke, and Kathryn saw and heard at Storyville is almost unrecognizable: though only forty-three, she is emaciated, her mouth puckered, and she has both the face and the carriage of a much older woman. Her voice, too, is shot, almost completely gone; it is so dry and hoarse that often, when she opens her mouth to sing, all that comes out is a rasp, a whisper. In short, she is a mere shadow of her former self, a dry husk, and she will die the following summer, at forty-four.

Now in the well-appointed living room of the Marlborough Street townhouse that Kathryn shares with Richard, seated in what is almost a circle of plush, overstuffed chintz armchairs, the three of them may as well still be in the club, as the sad, demoralizing effect of Holiday's dissolution pervades the atmosphere.

Kathryn lights a cigarette and turns to Starling: Do you think it's drugs?

He nods. Drugs, and everything else—drink and men and race and sex.... His voice trails off.

It's just so sad, Kathryn says.

I should know, Ling says, I was on my way.

Well, you look great now, Luke says, trying to turn the conversation around. Though I don't think it would hurt you to put on a few pounds.

Yes, you do look healthy, Kathryn adds, if slightly underfed.

Ling smiles and looks directly at both of them. Thanks. I feel good, too.

Good, Kathryn says, laughing. So let's have a drink, shall we? Brandy everyone?

Absolutely! Luke agrees.

Ling? Kathryn asks.

Sure, I'll have one, he says—for old time's sake.

Kathryn extinguishes her cigarette, gets up and walks over to the bar and begins opening cabinets, going about the business of making their drinks. Luke and Starling look at each other briefly but don't speak.

Kathryn breaks the heavy silence: What's so amazing to me, and what I think we always admired about her, or at least, speaking for myself, what I admired, one of the things, is that amid the seeming chaos of her personal life she was still able to create this style, to be an artist. And it was totally conscious. She pauses to shake the drink. You couldn't watch her, see her in person, and think that this was just some sort of spontaneous performance that she pulled out of nowhere: she knew *exactly* what she was doing.

Ling nods. Absolutely. And to see her do "Strange Fruit" bears out everything you're saying: her phrasing, her pacing, the pauses and the emphases—*everything*, down to the accompaniment on that song—lately it's been just her and the piano. Even the blue light she's bathed in. It's all a conscious choice. And that's artistry.

Luke sighs heavily: Can we talk about something else?

Ling and Kathryn both appear surprised.

It's not that I disagree, Luke says. It's just that—it's the story of so many artists, and it is so damn depressing. He looks up at the ceiling, as if searching for something, then he has a thought, turns to Kathryn: Tell us about those two girlfriends you're always mentioning.

Joanie and Mary Louise? Kathryn asks. She looks at Starling, as if for his approval of the change of subject, then she begins. Joanie's our age. Married. Tall and big-boned. Full of contradictions. Eccentric. Prickly, but funny as hell. She laughs, and then pauses to think. Mary Louise is ten years older—mid-forties, never married and not happy about it either. Born and raised in Brooklyn. Sad-looking, but even funnier than Joanie. Full of quips, and drier than the driest martini. She's a nurse. Kathryn raises her glass. You'll meet them while you're here. She pauses to light another cigarette, then turns to Luke: Do you think there are any happy artists?

Picasso? Ling interjects.

I don't think so, Luke says, looking at Kathryn. I think he's very angry and conflicted, full of rage.

Sorry, Ling, Kathryn says, but I'd have to agree with Luke on that one.

Luke laughs bitterly now: I can't think of a single writer.

Ling shakes his head: Me either. But how about somebody like Ella Fitzgerald?

Kathryn smiles: Well, she certainly makes everything *seem* happy, doesn't she?

Even the sad songs, right? Ling laughs.

It's true, says Luke, also laughing.

What about Colette? Kathryn chimes in, as if a light has gone on.

Hmm, Luke says. Interesting choice; I think you might be right.

And Monet? Kathryn adds.

I don't know much about his personal life, Luke says, but—Kathryn interrupts him, excited: And Matisse!

These are all French people, Ling says, laughing. Something tells me we're living in the wrong place.

Not that I can think of any other happy French writers, says Luke.

And after all, Jimmy Baldwin is there. And Josephine Baker....

As if moving and living elsewhere would solve all of our problems, Kathryn says knowingly. I think we've already been down that road.

Do you really think that's why we moved to Manhattan? Ling asks.

What do *you* think? she retorts.

He shrugs. I guess I think that had something to do with it.

Luke? Kathryn asks.

Definitely, he says. We were young, we were green—what did we know of the world?

Well, I agree with both of you, Kathryn continues: I do think the grass-is-always-greener syndrome did have something to do with it, but not everything. It was also just the mythic symbol of Manhattan, wasn't it? That great place we'd heard about and read about that was so alive and bustling and unlike anything we knew—

Ling interrupts: And here we are—or, there Luke and I still are.

Luke jumps in: And have been for—

Ling finishes his sentence:—For over twelve years now.

Kathryn is suddenly overcome with emotion: she is smiling but there are tears in her eyes. And are we happy? she asks. Or at least happier?

Definitely happier, Luke responds. Speaking for myself. He looks at his two friends. But all of this emphasis on happiness in American culture. It's so false and punitive; happiness is a transitory thing, not a permanent state. And yet we're raised to think that we're supposed to be happy all the time. He pauses and looks at Kathryn: If you're asking if we're glad we made the move—I am, yes, absolutely!

Ling sighs. This is a tough one for me, because things haven't exactly gone the way that I thought—and hoped—they would. He looks at both Kathryn and Luke. As you both know. And I feel like I got way off track for a while, so much so that at times I've wondered if I wouldn't have been better off just staying put. He shakes his head. But then I think—I couldn't live *there*. And so in the end I just wind up feeling betwixt and between, neither here nor there, and like I just haven't found the right place yet. He sighs again, heavily.

I'm sorry, Kathryn says to Ling, full of emotion. I guess I'm thinking that it's not really *place* we're talking about, but something else. She shakes her head as she lights another cigarette. I don't know: I remember my father, of all people—she laughs and rolls her eyes— my father used to say to me, 'Life has a funny way of throwing you a lot of curve balls, Katie.' She smiles at Luke and Starling. And I always hated it when he said that. But now, I'm almost embarrassed to admit that I know what he meant, because you do, in middle-age, start to find yourself in circumstances that you never thought you would be in—*ever*, and doing things that you never thought you would do, and…and yet there you are, in these situations, doing these things, because of…circumstances that have been handed to you, or because of things you've chosen or decisions you've made that haven't gone quite the way you thought they would. She looks at Starling intensely. But you're still the same person, just trying to make the best of things, to cope…. She is starting to lose control now. Or least you hope you are. And there's just something so sad about it all to me. She begins weeping openly. But this isn't just about me; I'm not crying only for myself: I think this is the human condition—that it's true for all of us.

Ling walks over to where Kathryn is sitting, kneels and puts his arm around her. Amen, sister! I know exactly what you're saying, and you said it a lot better than I ever could have.

Do you want to talk about it? Luke asks Kathryn quietly.

Still crying, and smoking, Kathryn shakes her head, and then laughs: No!

Well, at least you're honest, Luke chuckles ruefully.

And one of the questions you ask yourself, Ling says thoughtfully, looking at Kathryn, or that I repeatedly ask myself, is, after all of these experiences—if you really are and can be the same person you once were; can you have the same core, the same soul, or have you lost it, has it somehow been distorted or changed, permanently altered? I ask myself this all the time.

Kathryn nods: And the irony is, I think, that you find yourself wanting to be changed by the positive experiences—to learn and grow and become a better person, but not by the negative ones, or at least not in a negative way; not to be...warped or...perverted by them. And I guess that's just not realistic. She stares off into space for several moments, as the room remains quiet, then quotes: 'We poets in our youth begin in gladness \ But thereof come in the end despondency and madness.'

Your beloved Wordsworth, Luke says, looking at Kathryn. Go on—More! More!

Kathryn shakes her head, then turns to her friends, wistfully: Were we poets in our youth?

Aren't all children? Ling says sadly.

Luke gets up and walks toward the bar: I think we all need another drink. Kathryn? Ling? Both nod, and Luke begins pouring a second round. Somebody once said that Manhattan is an example of a city that yearns to belong to another country.

I love that! Kathryn laughs, as she puts out her cigarette, walks over to the window and looks down onto Marlborough Street. They should try living in Boston, an example of a city that yearns to belong to another century.

Luke laughs and winces. Oh, that's ripe, Kathryn!

Should we move? Ling asks.

Luke serves his friends their drinks: I like my job, he says, shaking his head. That's the funny thing; or, not funny but...I am actually fairly happy, all things considered.

How goes the analysis anyway? Kathryn asks.

Luke shrugs. It goes.

Everybody's doing it, Ling mock-sings, and then adds, Everybody who can afford it.

Seriously, Kathryn says, grim-faced.

Seriously, I think it's helped, Luke says slowly, clearly thinking before he speaks. It's helped me work through some things I needed to work through, like Laird's death—not that I think I'll ever get over that; like coming to terms with my mother and father....

How *are* your parents? Kathryn asks.

Nada y pues nada y pues nada.... Luke falls back on his standard response.

And has analysis helped you with anything else? Ling asks suggestively.

What do you mean? Luke wonders aloud, momentarily in the dark.

Ling immediately thinks better of his line of questioning and turns to Kathryn: And your parents?

Grateful for Ling's correction, Kathryn responds quickly. Mother's her usual self, which is to say a wonder. But Dad's not doing so well at all; his liver is shot. She pauses and rolls her eyes: *Quelle surprise*, right? She looks at Luke now, who is almost glaring at Ling, having belatedly understood the gist of his question. And Ermine? she asks Ling, hoping to steer the conversation away from a head-on collision.

Ling laughs nervously, happy for the opportunity to distract from his question to Luke. She's as ornery and as…as, well, *Ermine* as ever. I think I told you that she finally visited me—last fall I guess it was. And she *loved* New York. He begins imitating his mother: Why, honey, she just loved it. He laughs. I think she was waiting for me to invite her to move in with me.

It all comes back to where we come from, doesn't it? Luke says, happy to have avoided a confrontation. The place, the people—

Oh, I don't know, Kathryn jumps in. Then she yawns and lights yet another cigarette. I mean, yes and no—I do think there's something to be said for self-invention, that it is possible to a certain extent.

Artists do it all the time, Ling adds.

Not that any of us can be completely free of our pasts, Luke posits.

Kathryn shakes her head: No, I'm not saying that.

Ling takes center stage: But how else to explain how a little girl named Eleanora Fagan, who grows up in poverty in Baltimore and suffers all kinds of abuse, becomes the world-renowned artist known as Billie Holiday, a stylist of the first rank?

Kathryn yawns and nods her head in agreement.

And I guess maybe what distinguishes them from us, Luke says, is that they've got this inexplicable fire burning, this fierce passion that just rides over everything else.

I thought I had that passion, Ling says sadly.

Probably a lot of people think they have it, Ling, says Luke sympathetically, until push comes to shove.

Yeah, Ling agrees, I recognize that. And push certainly did come to shove.

Maybe that's why so many artists have such miserable lives, Kathryn says. Because of what you just said, Luke, about that passion riding over everything else.

It makes perfect sense, Luke adds. You know, Yeats said that the human intellect is forced to choose between perfection of the life or of the work.

Kathryn puts out her cigarette, which is only half smoked. And so the moral of the story is that we should all be more satisfied with our lives, and go to bed happy. She gets up and kisses each of them on the cheek: Good night you two; I'm so glad you're both here. Then she goes to her room.

I guess it is about that time, isn't it? Luke says suddenly, not wanting to be left alone with Starling. He feigns a yawn, then rises and begins walking toward his room. Goodnight, Ling.

Ling sinks down into the sofa disappointedly: 'Night, Luke.

[10]

Another weekend in Manhattan, but now—all these many years later—Luke is no longer afraid, and he knows just what to do with himself. He has become as solid and firmly planted, and as fierce, as those stone lions that guard the entrance to the Public Library. Now, the weekends are like an old friend come to town for a visit, and he always welcomes them with open arms.

On the weekends he gets up when he wakes up (not to the rude sound of an alarm), drinks a cup of coffee, dresses, and then walks the fifteen blocks up to the YMCA where he swims for an hour. He always waits to shower and shave there at the Y, after his swim; and then he'll breakfast out somewhere, usually at a quiet diner just down the street, where he is by now a regular (*Mr. Alding-ton,* Jimmy, the manager, always greets him with a discreet nod and a smile). After breakfast (which is typically a grapefruit, two eggs over easy, toast and coffee) and the *Times,* he'll head down to the office, which is like a haven on weekends, a safe haven. There, it is quiet (unlike the hectic workweek, with all of the noise—so many phones ringing, so many people coming and going) and he can get a lot accomplished. The project that he is currently most excited about is a book on Slavko Vorkapich, master of the kind of montage used so prevalently in films of the 1930s and '40s, such as the pages of a calendar flipping or falling away to indicate the passing of time, or the wheels of a train to show travel over a great distance, etcetera The photographs are amazing!

Luke will spend anywhere from two to four or maybe even as many as five hours in the office. Or, if for whatever reason he's sick of the office, which is not often—but perhaps there was an editorial meeting the previous week that didn't go particularly well, or maybe his current favorite book isn't selling, which does happen, though it is always disappointing, you just become accustomed to it after a while...if he cannot face another day in the office, he'll haunt the bookstores, one of his favorite things to do. He'll stroll over to the Strand—he can easily spend hours there and get lost in time, the place is so large and labyrinthine and *rich with books*; and then he might walk up to the Gotham Book Mart on 47th: there are so many great bookstores in Manhattan!

He loves books, absolutely *loves them*, with a passion that anyone in the publishing business *should* have. And there are so many production details—the dust jacket, the binding, the often embossed and gilded printing on the spine; the colored endpapers; the way a book smells when you first open it (like a crisp autumn day, he often thinks); the publisher's colophon; the weight and feel (the texture!) of the paper; the typeface *and the history of that typeface*; and how the ink *sinks* into the paper; the all-important title page, and the overall layout and design; the different editions of the same book; even the blurbs (who's blurbing whom), the author photo, and of course, most importantly, the prose and the story and the style—the writing itself....

When he's out, he'll almost inevitably run into one of his authors, or one of his former authors—in one of the bookstores he's haunting, or simply walking down the street in Chelsea, or in a restaurant or a bar; and then the two of them will go for a drink, or for lunch, or coffee or tea, or even dinner. And but for the very rare exception, he can only think of two at present, he is always glad to see them—always. They are his friends, however fleetingly; and he feels a love for and a protectiveness of them that he feels for very few people.

This is his life.

1964

Starling is on stage, in an acting class (yes, he has finally taken Luke's advice), delivering Tom's soliloquy from *The Glass Menagerie*. The material fits him perfectly, and he fits it, and he is nothing short of brilliant in the scene—not that anyone but the handful present will ever see it.

> *I didn't go to the moon, I went much further—for time is the longest distance between two places. Not long after that I was fired for writing a poem on the lid of a shoe-box. I left Saint Louis. I descended the steps of this fire-escape for a last time and followed, from then on, in my father's footsteps, attempting to find in motion what was lost in*

*space. I traveled around a great deal. The cities swept about
me like dead leaves, leaves that were brightly colored but
torn away from the branches. I would have stopped, but
I was pursued by something* (Starling pauses here briefly,
as if listening for something). *It always came upon me
unawares, taking me altogether by surprise. Perhaps it
was a familiar bit of music. Perhaps it was only a piece of
transparent glass. Perhaps I am walking along a street at
night, in some strange city, before I have found compan-
ions. I pass the lighted window of a shop where perfume is
sold. The window is filled with pieces of colored glass, tiny
transparent bottles in delicate colors, like bits of a shattered
rainbow. Then all at once my sister touches my shoulder. I
turn around and look into her eyes. Oh, Laura, Laura, I
tried to leave you behind me, but I am more faithful than
I intended to be! I reach for a cigarette, I cross the street, I
run into the movies or a bar, I buy a drink, I speak to the
nearest stranger—anything that can blow your candles out!
For nowadays the world is lit by lightning! Blow out your
candles, Laura—and so goodbye. . . .*

At the end of the scene, Starling is overcome with emotion. He knows
that he was good—he could feel it while he was doing it: he successfully plugged himself into the material, lost himself, or perhaps found
himself, he isn't quite sure which. But as he looks into the awed faces
of his classmates, and at the knowing and approving expression of
his teacher, who is nodding and applauding, he is also suddenly and
painfully aware of how few people witnessed his performance (for a
moment he had forgotten, had thought he was performing before a
large audience), aware, too—perhaps—of the impossibility, even the
futility, of such a career, for himself. He runs out of the theatre.

September 7, 2001

Time, the endless idiot, runs screaming round the world.
—Carson McCullers

T he only juncture at which time seems to stop is when one dies, but even then, it is not time that has stopped (it will go on and on), one has merely ceased to observe it. In fact, any means of making time seem other than what it is—that is, incessant and inexorable: sixty seconds in a minute (each second standing heir to the first), sixty minutes in an hour, twenty-four hours in a day, three-hundred sixty-five and one-fourth days per year, et cetera—is merely illusory.

Kathryn was now and had for a while been thinking a lot about time, both because she seemed to have a fair amount of it on her hands these days—she was often alone, by choice, especially during the day; she did not have a job that she had to leave her house to go to—but also because she was seventy-five, and most every day now she was aware of the finiteness of her life, of time as she knew it.

And yet, she could realistically have another twenty years, or more—the equivalent of her youth, in time, since longevity ran in the family: her mother, at ninety-four, was still alive, mobile and, most importantly, lucid. But one did not see twenty years at age seventy-five in the same way that one saw twenty years when one was young.

She had lived three-quarters of one century and into the beginnings of another, and she was, now, taking an inventory of time, or rather, of the effects of time. First and most importantly was her mind; it was still rock solid, dependable, and quick as ever: she was always right there, if not a step or two ahead of the rest (whereas Starling, with his low blood pressure, had always stayed just behind the beat, like Billie Holiday sang, but that was also a matter of style, his style). If she forgot or misremembered something, she didn't attribute it to encroaching senility or, worse, dementia, but to an overcrowding of the mind, and she took it as a signal. *Just let it go*, she'd tell herself lightly.

Her sense of humor remained not only intact—and thank God, too, because she'd needed it; it was better than ever, sharper, heightened, much looser and freer and more acute, though she had always loved to laugh—that was one of the things she and Luke always shared, especially in their later years together.

And her body? Though not too bad for its age, it had thickened a bit here and there, mostly around the waist; and of course gravity had its wicked way as well, but there were things that one could do, things one could wear, to disguise all of that. She was not one to complain.

Her legs were still good, slender and shapely—all of the walking she did took care of that. Out in public, she still wore her favorite style of shoes—two-inch heels with thin straps around the instep. Like a hooker, Luke used to tease. Whereas at home a pair of fluffies were usually her shoes of choice.

She got her shoulder-length hair marcelled at least once every few months; she liked it best after it had relaxed. Several years ago she had stopped dying it, much to the relief of some of her friends; but then she could not stand the steel-gray color that it turned, because it reminded her of pewter—no, she did not appreciate the New England connotation of pewter, because she'd done that, lived there, for a time, with Richard, and so she had resumed having it colored, as close to its original cinnamon color as could be bought.

And then there was her face. It was faded, yes—like a paper lampshade (dimming the brightness that was still inside), like parchment, faded and heavily wrinkled—she could thank all the years of smoking for that. Like Auden's was, or like Hellman's, later in their lives. Auden lived in the Village, on Cornelia, when she, Luke and

Starling had also lived there, and she used to see him, occasionally, on the street. And then later, after she had married Richard, she actually met Auden—he was such a wonderfully funny, eccentric and, of course, brilliant man; Richard absolutely revered him. Whereas Hellman, whom she also met once—well, she won't go there....

A wedding cake left out in the rain, someone famously remarked (perhaps it was Auden himself?), about Auden's and/or Hellman's older face. The same could be said about hers now, and she knew it and could even laugh about it: it was a map of ruin and decay—Miss Havisham's delight! But it was the visage through which she now saw life, and through which she was seen—an old woman sitting in a window, or passed by on the street. Ah, but then!—then, in the summer of life (again, and always, time was the great demarcator)...then her face, always shaped something like an upside-down triangle, had a certain piquant quality; and yet always, too, from the age of three on—she saw it herself, in the old photographs—she looked like a sage.

But this was not her story, or not exclusively her story—it was also the story of Luke, her best friend, and Starling, her other best friend, and about the times they lived through together. For over thirty years all three of them played with and around each other like a good trio; they interwove; they coexisted; they danced, in the same way that Coleman Hawkins so famously played *around* the melody of "Body and Soul". And though individually they may not have had such great lives, together, at least for a while...ah, together! Imagine an unusual flower with only three large petals, and in the center was the golden essence of those petals, and that was them—for a time. Then their trio became a duo. And then.... And now....

But all that was yesterday; that was then. Now, today, was ten, twenty-five, seventy years later; the year was 2-0-0-1, and she was, now, a solo act; she was one.

It was a beautiful September day, and among the many things she would do today was go for a walk in the park adjacent to the Upper West Side neighborhood that she had called home for the past oh-so-many years. She was also, now, today, this moment, writing this, and would be doing so over a brief period of time, an afternoon or three, because, compositionally at least, she wanted the classical unities of time and place, here and now. But by the time she finished this, of course, now would no longer be now, but then.

Between yesterday and today, now and then, life had intervened; and time was the great organizing principle—as if she could have had it any other way. And so she had chosen, wisely, she thought, to try to go with the flow; not to go gently was a waste of energy; Richard knew Dylan Thomas, and look what happened to him.

Yes, she was thinking a lot about time these days, just as her own was running out. She was thinking about the past and the present and the future, and about how, as children, we live mostly in the future—though sometimes also in the present—when we are playing imaginatively, intensely engaged in the moment; we live mostly in the future as children because we long to leap from the powerlessness of childhood into the power and autonomy of adulthood. And in old age, we live mostly in the past, not only because we see that the future is finite, and that death looms, but also because, in many if not most cases, the present is diminished—by illness, infirmity, the death of so many friends, et cetera And so it is in middle age that we have the greatest opportunity to live most fully in the present, in the moment; whether or not one chooses or is able to do so is up to the individual.

She did choose—once and for a while…. And here she writes about an interlude in her life, an interval, something that fell in the cracks, between the acts, when the curtain was down…. Her love affair with Peter was, always, very much in and of the present, the moment; it began in 1957 and lasted until his premature death in 1971. No one knew about them—no one, not Richard, not Peter's wife (as far as she knows), not Mary Louise or Joanie, not even Luke and Starling—though she did, very obliquely, allude to it once with them, in a conversation about the surprising turns our lives take as adults; no one knew. It was just between Peter and her, and that was how they both wanted it. It was theirs and theirs alone.

How did it begin? Easily, it was the easiest thing in the world—

not morally, she didn't mean morally; in fact, she was haunted by that particular question for years. Richard was often away, out of town, out of the country, promoting poetry (promoting himself—which, she eventually realized, poets must do), and he was also having his own (so she found out later) multitude of affairs. Peter and his wife lived in Wellesley and he drove into downtown Boston every day, a good half-hour drive, to the law firm on State Street.

And then one day she and Peter both happened to be sitting in the same luncheonette in the financial district, in a little place on Milk Street; she was down there doing business for Richard, managing his money, which was not at all unusual in those days. They were sitting there, she and Peter, waiting for their lunches, when their eyes met. And that was how it began. Their eyes met and, obviously, they connected, found something—some reflection or refraction or what have you—in each other's eyes. He smiled. She smiled back. And then they both—and she knew this because they had talked about it later—they both proceeded, very self-consciously, to eat their lunches; Peter told her later that she had nervously dabbed around her mouth a lot with the napkin. They ate their lunches, or pretended to, and they stole looks at one another (or they thought the looks were stolen), and this went on and on, it seemed, for an eternity; it was agonizing, but it was also, of course, completely delicious. And then there came a moment, a very confused and confusing moment, when Peter stood up: it seemed that he was coming over to her table; or was he merely getting up to leave? She couldn't be sure. But she panicked regardless, and something in her body language, he told her much later, something about the way she moved, how she appeared to be responding or reacting to his getting up, the slightest adjustment on her part, communicated to him, he said, that she was not interested. And so he walked right past her and made his way to the door: she could only imagine that she must have looked like a collapsed soufflé at that moment; that is certainly how she felt; her body had betrayed her. But then at the last minute, in the doorway, Peter turned around and looked at her one last time, and he caught her looking back at him; she had rallied quickly. He paused and smiled and, for just a brief moment, everything seemed to slow down, to occur in slow motion. But then it speeded up again, as someone walked in the door on the other side; and then, too, suddenly somebody else was standing behind Peter, waiting to exit, and instead of stepping aside, Peter walked out—out the door, outside, and out of her life. And that, apparently, was that.

Except that it wasn't—because she thought about Peter again and again, not without some guilt, in the days that followed, and he (he later told her) also thought about her, in an equally obsessive fashion. And then, unbeknownst to each other, they both began plotting their next moves: how could they meet again? After a couple of days' contemplation at home, Kathryn went downtown and began walking around in that area from noon to two PM. She felt like a streetwalker!—State Street, Federal Street, School Street; fortunately, it was spring (May), so the weather was conducive. And of course she went back to the luncheonette, too. Whereas Peter, he told her later, returned to the luncheonette the very next day, and at the same time, too—he was so logical. But then, he told her he had thought afterward, that *that* was much too obvious, and she (he had decided), she would be anything but obvious, which was, he later told her, one of the things he initially liked about her, or rather his fantasy of her, since that was before they had even met.

And so there they both were, in downtown Boston, in the financial district during the busy lunch period, amid what was surely thousands of people every day—lawyers and stockbrokers and clerks and jewelers and merchants and shoppers and tourists—looking for each other, two people who did not draw attention to themselves, and who would not necessarily stand out in a crowd: ah, but she had quickly figured that out and begun wearing her red hat! And then finally, before a full week had passed, though not before a seemingly endless weekend had intervened, a weekend as long as a year, on the sixth day since they first sat across from each other in the luncheonette, she and Peter saw each other again, and this time they decidedly met, and spoke. They ran into each other on the street.

There you are, Peter said boldly.

She was stunned. There she was, indeed, and there he was. But—Yes, was all she could manage to say in response.

I have been looking for you, he said, a sly smile playing across his face.

Yes, was again all she could say, by which she meant of course, that she had been looking for him, too; but how could he know that?

That is a very nice hat, he said, and winked.

She was sure she must have blushed then—he had found her out!

But before she reveals the rest of what happened between them that day, let her describe him as they stood there in the middle of the sidewalk along busy State Street, amid the throng of passersby.

He was handsome, yes, but not obviously so; he was not a pretty boy. Rather, his was a mature handsomeness. But that's abstract: let her start over. A wide face with high cheekbones that she came to enjoy tracing the contours of with her fingers or her lips. Blue eyes that looked both hurt and wise—cold, seawater blue. Dark brown, almost black hair—always a startling contrast to blue eyes—a long lock of which was constantly falling down across his forehead and into his eyes, and which he frequently and habitually swept away with his right hand. A long, sharp nose, and perfectly shaped, full, sensual lips. Broad shoulders, and he was tall, too—six feet plus, and in good condition; but probably more importantly, in terms of how he appeared, was that he carried himself with such dignity, had such a strong bearing; and he also dressed well—he was wearing a scarf that first day, not a woolen winter scarf, but a silk scarf, burgundy, and she decided that he was either European or affected. In short, like Richard when she first met him, Peter cut quite the romantic figure; and also like Richard, she supposed, looking back, there *was* something doomed about Peter, though that did not register with her at the time.

Would you like to have lunch with me? he asked, as they stood there together that day on State Street.

She nodded, and so they proceeded to walk—or should she say

that they (or she) proceeded to float?—in awkward silence toward the luncheonette on Milk Street where they had first seen one another; somehow, and in some way, it was as if they both already knew that their ultimate destination would eventually be each other's arms, in a bed somewhere.

But there in the crowded luncheonette, finally seated—for which she was grateful, since her legs, and in particular her knees, felt weak, they introduced themselves.

Peter Reinmann, he said, and she thought, not for the first time, that she detected a slight accent. It was then, too, as he folded his beautifully veined hands on the table, that she first noticed his wedding ring.

German? she asked.

He nodded, but seemed to want to brush the subject aside, not to allow any follow-up, as he quickly asked, You?

Kathryn, was all she could say. She did not at that point want to reveal her last name; but then she laughed and added, Irish.

And so they ordered and ate their lunches, or rather he ate his lunch—she could only nibble that day; a bite or two was the most she could manage to digest, because she felt so unnerved in Peter's presence. And this calls for yet another digression of sorts.

Before Peter, sex, for her, had never been anything much, which was to say that she had never especially enjoyed it or looked forward to it; somehow that particular spark had never been ignited between her and Richard—no, their connection was primarily intellectual. She certainly didn't experience sex as the be-all, end-all that it was touted to be—this, during a time when Freud (*read sex*) was all the rage. To her, it had always seemed so...mechanical—the laborious undressing (or not undressing); the man climbing on and off; all of the cute little non-verbal cues that the lovers were supposed to signal and pick up on and heed...she found it tiresome. And disingenuous. And messy—even dangerous. And it seemed to her, too, to yield so very little pleasure or reward for so much effort. Sex had often struck her as either terribly sad—it frequently left her feeling that way—or occasionally, as hysterically funny, depending upon one's partner and how very seriously he took it and *applied himself.* And yet it was clearly and undeniably sex that was on the table between her and Peter that day in the luncheonette; it was on the table between them, and in the space around them, it was in the very air—suddenly, sex was every-where. It was so pervasive, in fact, and the atmosphere around them so charged, that it was clearly not a matter of *if* she and Peter would come together, but when, and how, and where, and she believed that everyone else in the luncheonette that day could see this as well.

And so it was mostly a painfully silent and rattling lunch, that first day, with the two of them sending soulful, darting glances across the table to each other, their eyes occasionally meeting and locking, however momentarily, and their bodies straining toward the other, as if the law of gravity was horizontal, not vertical, and applied only to them—or that was how she experienced it. On the surface of the table, their hands played with their food, dallied with the condi-ments, danced and skittered and chased, unwittingly, the hands of the other—anything just to touch, to connect. It was delirious tor-ture, long and laborious foreplay.

But nothing more happened between them that day. Peter finished his lunch and asked if she had finished hers, then suddenly announced that he had to get back to the office for a meeting. She was stunned, until he followed up with a question: might he see her again? Her eyes on his the entire time, she said yes without even hesi-tating, and so they worked out the particulars of where and when, and then he took her hand, kissed it, and said goodbye.

Looking back now, she knew that Peter was far too much of a gentleman to suggest that they go to bed immediately that first day, but at the time she was surprised, and also disappointed.

And so that was how it began, how they began—ordinarily, she supposed, like many, if not most, love affairs. The next time they met—same time, same place—after lunch Peter suggested that they go to a hotel for the afternoon, which they did; and there they made love until it grew dark out, at which point Peter said that he had to go. They didn't talk much at all that first time, nor did they seem to do much talking for the first few weeks, really; neither of them even

knew for sure that the other was married, though both wore wedding rings. She supposed they both felt they didn't need to talk, or
didn't especially want to talk; instead, what they wanted, and what
they did, was devour each other for as long as they had—an hour or
two or four, depending.

She had long relished the phrase *love in the afternoon*, and
that was what she and Peter had—for more than fourteen years, they
always met only in the afternoon.

Love affairs, by necessity she supposed, and perhaps also by
definition, always take place in the present tense—whatever time
the lovers can grab, the caught moment here or there, the *now*, as
they light into one another...—and she believed that both she and
Peter knew that, respected it, valued it, and were grateful for it; and
so before even beginning to bother getting to know one another, to
explore each other's pasts, or to discuss the future—at that point they
had neither the time nor the mind, and it would be months before
they did—they got to know one another, for the most part, non-ver-
bally, carnally; often, the most they could manage to say before beginning to make love was, How are you? And from that they developed
a very strong bond, of sorts, and she had always been very proud of
that, by which she meant—proud of herself in particular, that she
was able to do it, capable of it. But eventually, and naturally, she and
Peter were curious: who was this person with whom they were shar-
ing their bodies and spending these deeply intense and passionate
afternoons? And so, very slowly, and gradually, they started talking
and getting to know one another in new ways. After a year or so they
began to spend whole afternoons doing nothing but talking—not
that the fire had gone out of their relationship; that never happened.
The content of those conversations might range from the quotidian—everything that had occurred since the last time they had seen
each other and up until the very moment they met that day—to
their background and biography, or to a memory of or an incident
from childhood; it suddenly seemed that there was so much to know
and learn, so many things to catch up on. And what was especially
wonderful was that both she and Peter were deeply interested; they

weren't just feigning interest so that they could get to the sex—they didn't have to, they'd had that.

But over the period of fourteen years, there were also many interruptions, long stretches of time, even whole seasons—when she and Richard were in Manhattan, for example (often, against the grain, they spent their summers there), or when they were traveling; and there were times when Peter simply couldn't get out of the office, or weeks when he was away on vacation with his wife—long dry spells when she and Peter did not because they could not, see one another. But then they always came back together again, easily, and comfortably, but never so comfortably that they took one another for granted, or that it got boring. Never. She even gave up cigarettes for him.

Over time, she learned that Peter was the only child of very distinguished parents: his mother, Elke, was Swiss, and a physician—he always described her as a very beautiful woman, which Kathryn could easily believe, looking at Peter. And his father, Herman, nineteen years older than his mother, was a German Jew, and a distinguished professor of philosophy. The family had lived in Frankfurt, and Peter portrayed a surprisingly sunny childhood, saying that though his parents probably sounded, because of their professions and intellects, cold and forbidding, they were actually quite the opposite—very warm and fun-loving people who had made it their business to know how best to raise a child. And they had done a marvelous job too, he would add, smiling wistfully, *hadn't they?*—to which she would nod her head and say, Yes, indeed they had.

His parents had wanted more children, Peter said—a brother and a sister for him to play with, his mother told him—but that was not to be. And when it became clear that it was not to be, Peter said that his parents did their very best to fill in the gap left by the absence of a brother or sister, welcoming his cousins as well as children from the neighborhood into their house, and allowing Peter to go and spend time in their homes, as much as possible.

They were such intelligent and freethinking people, Peter said, that in his teenage years—when he was attending the venerable Goethe Gymnasium—he felt very little need or desire to rebel against them or their ideas, and so the transition in their relationship, from dependent child-parent to independent...friends, was smooth and seamless.

It was an idyll, Peter would say of his childhood time and time again, and perhaps it seemed even more so because of what followed.

In January 1933, Peter's father, who was not only a Jew and a philosopher, but also a socialist, was arrested by the Nazis and imprisoned. But because a few of Elke's longtime patients also happened to be nominal members of the Nazi party, they willingly intervened for her on his behalf, and miraculously and fortunately, Herman Reinmann was released after only one month in prison—Peter explained that such things were still possible during the early years of the Third Reich. But his parents also saw the writing on the wall, and they insisted that Peter leave Germany immediately: he could go to Amsterdam, his father suggested, live with relatives and attend the university there. And so several weeks later, after encountering many bureaucratic obstacles, Peter finally succeeded in obtaining a passport, and then on February 27, 1933, the very day the Reichstag went up in flames, he fled Frankfurt for Amsterdam. The Reinmanns assured him that they would follow when and if they could. But Peter never saw them again.

She could still remember the very moment that Peter told her about his parents: they were at the hotel, lying in bed; it was late in the afternoon, when the body's energy always seems to flag. Daylight was also dying, and suddenly everything felt terribly drained and diluted: a tear slid from the corner of his eye and onto the palm of the hand in which his head was propped.

In Amsterdam, Peter said, he lived for a time with a distant cousin, a widower, and attended the university, which he completed in three years. Then he entered law school. And it was there that he met the two people he would always refer to as his best friends for life, Renate, who was Dutch, and Hans, a German refugee like himself, both law students, and both also Jewish. Mere months after their first meeting, Peter said, the three of them became inseparable.

They were competitive, each trying to out-study and out-perform the other—especially in formal debates or while arguing the mock trials often held as part of the curriculum; and yet they also relished each other's triumphs. Renate, Peter said, was petite and delicate-looking, like a piece of fine china—Dresden; but she had a ferocious intelligence, too, he added, as evidenced by her high forehead. Whereas Hans was a big man—tall and stocky, with a mind that was the most strictly logical Peter had ever encountered: So logical that it could be maddening!

Those too, like my childhood, were golden years. Peter paused and looked at Kathryn, then added, But they were also tarnished by the very reason I was there in Amsterdam and not in Frankfurt with my parents. He sighed. I knew at the time that those years were special, and I treasured them as fully as I knew how.

As Peter paused to take a sip of the wine they were drinking, a delicate Riesling he had brought along, she looked at him in the dim light that was left in the room; he had asked her earlier not to turn on the bedside lamp. She could barely see him, and so to reassure him that she was there, listening, and that she loved him, she smoothed his forehead with her hand, and then she lifted that same lock of hair that he was always lifting himself and brushed it back onto the top of his head. But as soon as he moved, however slightly, the recalcitrant lock fell down over his forehead again and over one eye. He went on.

It was as if we were in love, all three of us with the other. And yet nothing sexual ever took place. We simply...enjoyed each other's company—immensely. But by late 1940, when all three of us had finally completed law school—we finished at different times, myself in the spring of 1939, Renate that fall, and Hans, who finished last, one year later—by that time the Nazis were already issuing their first anti-Jewish decrees in Amsterdam, and Renate, Hans and I saw that it would be an impossible time to try to find a job. But what to do?

Peter sighed as if reliving the dilemma, and then he took another sip of wine. Before we could really gather our wits, in March of the following year the Nazis issued the decree that prohibited

Jews from traveling. And though we discussed trying to escape—we had heard that certain places in Switzerland were a safe haven—we decided, all three of us, together, that it would be unwise, too risky, and that we should probably just stay in Amsterdam. And so that is what we did—and Hans and Renate moved in with me at my cousin Gustav's, who was not Jewish.

It was now after five, when Peter usually had to leave, and as he looked at the clock on the bedside table, he announced that he would have to go. It is probably for the best, he added, as I cannot go on just now anyway. He sighed deeply: I will finish telling you another time.

What Peter told her.

He said that he and Renate and Hans didn't leave his cousin's house for over two years, and that Gustav was nothing less than a guardian angel to them the entire time, providing them with everything he possibly could—and then some, and at great risk to himself, too. Peter said that he, Renate and Hans all lived in one room, in which there were two beds, one of which he and Hans had to share. It was there that they talked about the future, which Peter said all three of them fervently continued to believe in, and were certain they would have. All three planned to go to America as soon as it was safe to do so: Renate said she wanted to live and work in Manhattan, and to attend concerts at Carnegie Hall; Hans preferred Los Angeles, California, and told his friends that he dreamed of meeting Marlene Dietrich. They were still young and foolish at times, and sometimes they argued and fought—like anybody else; or like any three people cramped into one room for two years, Peter would add. Most of the time, he said, they got along very well, and they talked and played cards and read and discussed whatever books Gustav could procure for them; and of course they talked, too, about Hitler's ultimate defeat and the end of the war. But they also, all four of them, worried constantly about being caught, each of them some days more than others: had the spoon accidentally falling on the floor given them away? Had someone Gustav knew, who also happened to know that he didn't eat eggs, seen him buying eggs? Or had one of them been seen by the wrong person when Renate accidentally brushed the heavy curtains aside as she was making the beds…it was ridiculous! The worry was constant. And demoralizing. It ate away at you, Peter said. It was a horrible way to live. But, he added in a choked voice, it was life, we were alive.

But then, early one afternoon in late 1943, it was November—somehow (Peter said he never found out how) they were discovered: several SS officers stormed the apartment, and all three of them, along with Gustav, were rounded-up and immediately deported to Westerbork, a transit camp that had been set up until transport to Auschwitz was possible.

Peter told Kathryn that he never saw Renate again. And that much, much later, he learned that she had died of starvation in Auschwitz.

Whereas he actually saw Hans from time to time, Peter said, after they were transferred to Auschwitz in January of 1944, though not consistently, and never again after September of that year.

What I eventually learned, he went on, was that there were several attempts by prisoners to escape from Auschwitz—this was in October of 1944—and Hans was either killed during, or as a result of having participated in, one of those attempts.

Peter stopped and looked at her, and then, as if anticipating her next question, said: Gustav, too, died at Auschwitz. Poor, innocent Gustav, who would not have been there were it not for me, Peter hung his head. And then, just a few months later—as ironical as life often is—the Russian troops came in, and the camp was liberated.

That was as far as Peter would go—he wouldn't talk about life in Auschwitz itself; he said that he just could not do it, though Kathryn tried, periodically, to encourage him to talk about it, saying that she thought it would help and might even be good for him. He would just shake his head, and once he had even snapped at her—Good for me?!—as if she hadn't a clue; and she supposed she hadn't.

But then one time, when Peter probably had too much wine, he began saying, as if in a trance, that perhaps Kafka had somehow been prescient, because it was as if he, Peter, had gone to sleep the night before as himself, as Peter Reinmann. But then when he woke up the following morning, he was in the camp and had become a mere…cockroach. An insect. A nothing.

Now, Peter's eyes turned the coldest shade of blue she ever saw them. Suddenly, he said, we were all living this sub-human existence, and so many of us, including me, became sub-human ourselves.

He stared off into space, blankly, coldly, and then he continued. There was this man there, Rudolf, about my age, young. He was a homosexual, and I hated him—not because he was a homosexual, so much, but because he had sold himself, had made a deal with the *kapo*—*kapos* were prisoners, usually camp elders, who were charged with ensuring obedience and discipline in the barracks. Peter sighed, and seemed to burrow even further into himself, into the past.

Rudolf performed sexual favors for the *kapo* and God only knew who all else, in exchange for extra food rations and exemption from arduous work assignments. He kept saying to me, over and over, *I'm going to stay alive. I'm going to live.* How I hated him! While I and most of the others survived on soup, which some of the veterans referred to as shoe-water, or the occasional sardine or potato, Rudolf enjoyed a wide variety of foods. And while the rest of us performed such demoralizing tasks as carrying large stones from one pile to another and then back again—meaningless, back-breaking work—Rudolf did no work at all. I despised him. And yet—Peter stared off into the distance; then he hung his head. Once, it was near the end of winter, and at the end of the long day—we worked for twelve hours, with a three-minute break every two hours. I was so tired. And cold. Exhausted and hungry. And there was Rudolf, sitting on his cot, eating—or I should say savoring—a link of sausage.

Peter stopped, looked Kathryn in the eyes: I was so tired and cold and famished; out of my right mind. And so just after Rudolf finished eating the sausage, I went over to him—as if automatically, or unconsciously—I went over to him, knelt at his feet, and licked every finger of the hand that had so recently held the sausage. Fingers that had been God only knew where! And Rudolf had a sick smile on his face the entire time.

Now Peter's head fell forward, as he added, his voice raised: And I had thought that being shaved, stripped and de-loused was humiliating! This was worse, because I had humiliated myself. It was disgusting; *I* was disgusting.

He looked up at her again. It wasn't until many years later that I really thought about Rudolf and the desperate situation he had been in. He was just trying to survive, like all of us. And I am sure it was even worse for him, being homosexual. Peter sighed again: I was wrong to hate him. And that is what I mean about having been so dehumanized....

He shuddered, and then he stopped, just like that; and it turned out to be the only time in over fourteen years that he ever said anything to her about life in the camp. Kathryn would never forget it, though, because it was so graphic, and because it made her wonder the very same thing about Kafka that Peter had the notion that his work was prescient—among so many other things. And suddenly, too, she believed that she finally understood that complex look in Peter's eyes, a gaze that appeared both hurt and all-knowing, all-seeing: he had truly been to hell and back.

But sensing that he wanted more than anything to move on, that he didn't want her to respond to or ask any questions about what he'd just told her, she had to ask, finally, fearing the worst: But what about your parents?

They never left Frankfurt. He shook his head sadly. My father, I found out later, got cancer and died in 1942. And my mother...he paused and stared off into space. No one seems to know, he shrugged: It is as if she vanished into the very air. He made a helpless gesture with his hands. Of course I tried to find her for quite a long while; I contacted people who knew her, I did everything I could think of, but no one had any information, or if they did, they would not tell me. So then I retraced her steps, as much as possible. After a while, the trail would either go cold or it would end up leading me to where it had started, back to our old house in Frankfurt.

Peter looked at Kathryn, incredulous once more: I did everything humanly possible! I checked the records of all the camps; I looked up the city's death certificates.... His voice faded. There was nothing.

She didn't know what to say. So what do you think?

I do not know what to think! he pounced. She is clearly dead—but how? Where? When? He shook his head again. I don't know. He gazed down into some invisible abyss and said sadly: I can only hope that she did not suffer too much. He stared off into space again, at some seemingly fixed horizon line: "We are accustomed to see men deride what they do not understand, and snarl at the good and beautiful because it lies beyond their sympathies."

Goethe, he added. And then he looked at her intently: I really tried, Katrina.

And she said, wanting to reassure him, that she believed him, she knew he must have done absolutely everything that he possibly could.

Peter said that by the time he learned how truly alone he was—that he had lost not only his best friends but also his parents and his cousin, among so many others—which was in mid-1946, by that time he was so devastated, so out of his mind with grief, that he felt that he just had to get out of Europe as soon as possible, no matter what; he said it was all he could think about, the only thing he wanted: he was obsessed.

And so he made plans to travel to America, and by the end of the year he was cruising into New York Harbor, with that impressive, daunting skyline in the background, rising up into what was on that day a brooding sky. He said that he had immediately thought of Renate, of course, because of her desire to move to New York City, and that for a while he felt as though he had to live there *for her*, to live the life that she could not live, that she had been denied. But though there was a small émigré community, situated in Washington Heights, Peter said that at the time the city was simply too much for him—too noisy and too busy, and there were far too many people, and all of it was much too soon. But it was there that he met up again with Martin Dankner, his boyhood rival at the Gymnasium. Dankner had a friend who worked at a law firm in Boston. So Peter moved to the Boston area. The friend of Dankner's who was a partner in the law firm, Stephan Schuetz, took Peter under his wing, and directed Peter towards taking a second degree at Harvard Law—because only then, Schuetz told Peter, would he be able to practice in the States.

And that is how I came to be here, Peter said. I began as a lowly clerk and worked my way up. Eventually, I decided that it would be through my career that I could best honor Renate and Hans. He paused, looked down. And along the way I met and married my wife.

But they did not talk about his wife—ever, nor did they talk about Richard (not then, anyway); she didn't think either of them especially wanted to know; or perhaps it would be more accurate to say that they both wanted to know about the other's spouse but did not want to have to talk about their own; she knew that was certainly true for her. Though she did tell him all about her best friends, Luke and Starling, just as he had told her about Renate and Hans.

And so she and Peter went on and on, for almost fifteen years, and over time she came to feel that she knew him in the way that one knows a character in a book, which—as she once said to him, and as has been better and more famously said by others (E. M. Forster, for example)—is often deeper and more intimately than one knows one's friends. There were so many other people in each of their lives that they saw more frequently and for longer periods of time than they were ever able to see each other, but the time that she and Peter did spend together was so intense and concentrated, so undiluted—they were paying the fiercest possible attention to each other; and it was for the most part regular and frequent, too, for over fourteen years. It was wonderful, and it was all hers: Peter had come along at just the right time in her life—not only when she needed someone, but also at a time when she could allow herself to have him.

But then that terribly hot and impoverished day in July of

1971 when she learned that Peter had been killed—by reading his obituary in the *Boston Globe* (hit by a car while crossing the street in Wellesley)—that day was one of the saddest days of her life, because it was the end not only of Peter, and of what they had together, what they shared, but also because it marked the end of a whole era of her life: she was forty-six, and she suddenly realized it, was forced to acknowledge the fact that so much of her good life was behind her—or so she thought at the time. Richard had also died by then, prematurely, from a heart attack, in 1968, though he had moved out in '64 and married his much younger girlfriend (Carolyn was twenty-four years his junior). Starling had been gone for six years. Her father was dead. Her friend Mary Louise had been diagnosed with ovarian cancer in '70 and died less than a year later, just a few months before Peter's sudden death. And much to her surprise—no, she had never fully accepted it as her fate—she had no children, and now it was too late.

And so for a while after Peter's death she did absolutely nothing at all, nothing but sit around that damned insufferable townhouse on Marlborough Street that she'd never liked, unable, really, to grieve, yet feeling sorry for herself. But the time was not completely fallow, as it was then, too, that she consciously went about imprinting and making indelible certain memories of Peter; she had no photographs. For example—his lifting the lock of hair that continually fell onto his forehead and into his eyes with those long, distinguished fingers of his; or how, just before he left their hotel room, Peter would always look in the mirror and knot the scarf or ascot he was wearing.

She also made sure that she would be able to remember the particular quality of his voice, the timber—that she could hear it, its specific resonance as he said her name; he always called her Katrine or Katrina. And something else that she adored about him: though they rarely left the hotel room, occasionally they would go out—to a bar or a restaurant in downtown Boston—and whenever they did and there happened to be a man wearing a hat at table, which happened not infrequently, Peter would absolutely implode, going on and on—though always only to her—about how rude and uncivilized it was, especially in the presence of a lady. She supposed it was the Old World European in him, and it was charming and something that she never failed to enjoy: Peter was nothing if not gallant.

She had remained in Boston all those years, post the separation from Richard, mostly because of Peter, but now that he was gone she couldn't stand the thought of staying on. So she put the townhouse on the market, packed up, said good riddance to Boston, and returned to New York City—by then she owned the townhouse on Central Park West. But in leaving Boston, she also left behind Joanie, though of course they still saw one another from time to time—Joanie would reluctantly come to visit her in New York, or, more often, Kathryn would go back to Boston to see Joanie.

Joanie was always prickly. But ever since her husband Jay died (she was only in her late thirties at the time), she had mostly stayed in her apartment with the drapes closed, day in, day out, listening to opera, and crying. And yet Joanie could be hysterically funny, too: she still loved to sing bawdy songs. But now when Kathryn visited, Joanie was usually wearing some sort of caftan, and a turban, because (she said) she just couldn't be bothered to get dressed and do her hair; and it was just so fitting, too, because she finally looked the part that she had long performed—that of an imperious Russian princess! But it hadn't been the same since Kathryn moved back to New York, never again the same between her and Joanie, though Kathryn loved her dearly.

Thus began the second, or third...or fourth act of Kathryn's friendship with Luke. There had been a time when she and Luke seemed to drift apart. Looking back, she thought that Starling's disappearance had discombobulated them, had shaken them up in so many ways, not only because of how bizarre it was to experience someone just seeming to drop off the face of the earth, but also because the configuration had always been that of a trio—Kathryn, Luke, and Starling. But then all of a sudden it was as if she and Luke had to figure out how to be with each other alone and without the possible, dominating presence of Starling, which was always considerable, and that took both of them some time. And while she had no doubt that she and Luke had continued to think of the other as a close friend, she also believed that the fact that they lived in different cities eventually took its toll. One of the things that she had learned in this long life was that space was like time, in that there was something immovable and unchangeable, even destructive, about it, especially when combined with time: distance really did matter.

But then just as soon as she moved back to the City, she and Luke took up with each other again effortlessly, as if they were simply continuing an unfinished conversation, which in essence they were, since by then they had been talking to one another for some forty years. And so they caught up—as much as anyone can ever catch up (the phrase itself suggested the impossible—cheating time); and over the next twenty years, she and Luke grew as close as two friends could be: they saw each other all of the time—often twice a week or more—and when they weren't together, they were frequently on the telephone with each other. And she loved Luke dearly, and she knew he loved her. And yet…. Well, and yet, he didn't know about Peter, for example, not then; she hadn't told him, which—especially in the early days after Peter's death and her return to New York—was extremely difficult to do, or not to do, since it probably would have been helpful to be able to talk to someone, and that was certainly both her desire and her inclination in those days. But she stifled it; she just couldn't do it, she could not tell anyone. It just didn't feel right then, especially (ironically) now that Peter was gone and she was unable to ask for his opinion, or his consent. Nor did Luke tell her about himself and others, if, in fact, there were or had been others (she didn't know)—whether then or in the many years he had lived in New York City alone. In fact, during those very rare times when she and Starling had been alone together, just two or three occasions in the years before he disappeared, this was one of the things they always discussed: was Luke seeing anyone special? Perhaps instead of just one, he was going out with two or even three—or more!—different women; maybe he most enjoyed playing the field. Or was he dating men? Had he, in fact, over the years, been seeing anyone?

Starling told her that he had seen Luke out on the street a few times, with both men and women, which, as she pointed out to him, proved absolutely nothing; they could have been friends, or colleagues. Or, most likely of all, was Luke simply married to his job? She did not have a clue and she did not ask, nor did he tell her. That was how it could be, even with the closest of friends.

Ah, but those years between her and Luke—their late for-ties and fifties, even into their sixties—those years were truly sweet; and it gradually became fairly clear to her that Luke was not seeing anyone, though she supposed one could never be completely sure. Perhaps, like her with Peter, Luke had a secret love? She didn't know. But *now*, during those sweetened years, the honeyed autumn leaves of their lives, she and Luke always had a date—for cocktails, dinner, the theater; he was someone with whom she felt completely com-fortable and could always talk easily. Add to all of that the fact that Luke was still handsome—yes, he had aged well; that certainly did not hurt. Both of them purely delighted in each other's company during those years; all of the *sturm und drang* of youth was long gone, they didn't have to worry about money, and they were both able to fully enjoy life and live in the present, the moment. Kathryn did not want to talk about the past, did not want to talk about her marriage, and she did not want to talk about Peter; and Luke seemed to feel the same way—though they did, both of them, still feel the need, the desire even, to talk about Starling from time to time and to try to understand what may have happened to him. Luke would go over and over his conversations with the police, how they'd said they searched Starling's apartment, interviewed neighbors, contacted his family…that there were no signs of foul play.

You have to understand that this sort of thing is not all that uncommon around here. It happens all the time in this part of the city, a cop had told Luke. *People just up and disappear.* Which Luke told Kathryn at the time he understood to mean that it was Harlem and the police just couldn't be bothered.

Foul play. Suicide. Or somebody just walking away from their life, the staff sergeant said to Luke the last time he spoke with the police, some two years after Starling's disappearance. *He'll probably turn up in the East River eventually.*

Kathryn was still living in Boston then, but she traveled to the city several times to see what she could do to help; she had even used Richard's name. All to no avail.

Luke tried to stay on top of things, to pressure the police and to keep Kathryn informed. Months passed. Then years—until six years later she moved back to Manhattan, where she and Luke took up together again, and she suggested that they change their conversation about Starling to trying to imagine how he would have aged (quite well, they deduced), and what he would have been like *now*. Kathryn told Luke that she'd prefer to focus on the *what ifs*: what if Starling had found work in the theater or in movies, how different things might have been for him—because he was a natural born performer; what if he had been able to express himself and be appreciated for it? He might have soared. Sometimes, she added, she imagined that Starling had gone to Europe—and stayed, and that one day he would just show up again.

And once during that time, Luke had phoned, uncharacteristically excited, to tell her he had just learned that one of his first-time authors had been in an acting class with Starling, and the fellow said that Starling had been absolutely brilliant in a scene from *The Glass Menagerie.*

That's lovely, she said, fighting back tears.

Small world, isn't it? Luke said sadly, also clearly moved.

Usually, though, their talk was all about, What's new? How was your day? What are you doing, working on? What's happening *now?* Luke was still a Senior Editor at Farrar, Straus (Giroux had since been added), which was by then considered to be one of the more prestigious publishing houses in the U.S. And she, ironically, was being kept busy in those days as the literary executor of Richard's estate, busier than she had been ever since—no, he had not bothered to change his will. Once, on the telephone—this was after he had been living with Carolyn for a while—he told Kathryn that there was no one that he trusted more than her; and really, there was no ire between them at the end, they had mellowed, and she did love him and felt, always, a terrible sadness about his life and all that he had endured. She was, in fact, stunned and terribly saddened by his sudden death in '68; their connection was undeniable. She didn't know what she would have done during that time without Peter, because it was then, finally, when she learned of Richard's death, that she just had to talk to Peter about him, and so she did—about their marriage and about Richard's illness and some of the terrible scenes she had witnessed and been through with him over the years, and about his work and how much she admired it, and about his family, and all that the two of them had shared over the years; and finally, at bottom, telling Peter that there was a good and very decent man buried underneath all of the *rubbish* that was Richard's illness, which made his life something of a tragedy, she thought.

Hell hath no fury like a famous poet's wife, Anatole Broyard wrote so amusingly about Caitlin Thomas, Dylan Thomas's wife, in his memoir *Kafka was the Rage*. Well, that was her; and besides, Kathryn was a famous poet's *ex* (even though they'd never bothered to divorce). So yes, she was kept especially busy as the executor of Richard's literary estate in those days, dealing with biographers and hagiographers and anthologists and reprint permissions and copyrights, et cetera et cetera et cetera *ad infinitum*, while also still trying to write a book herself (unbeknownst to anyone but her mother), which she had picked up and put down as many times as there had been years—if not more, in the past twenty or so. It was a lifelong dream of hers, to write a book: was she simply supposed to let it go, the way that so much else had somehow gone? She thought not.

And so she and Luke went on, together, and those were very interesting years in America, too—unlike the mean time of the fifties. Though this was 1972—and later—for a while the mores of the sixties were still in effect, still having their say, their day, and she and Luke had something of a last hurrah, she supposed it was, for the next ten years or so—for as long as they could get away with it, as they both approached, and then left behind, age fifty. They went out dancing at least once a week, having recently discovered that both of them loved to dance but had no one to go out dancing with all those years. They even made it into Studio 54 once, somehow—through someone Luke knew in publishing who knew someone else who… that was truly a *fin de siécle* experience. And oh how Luke—a die-hard liberal, and a Stevenson supporter (as he was always so quick to remind anyone and everyone)—how he relished the Watergate Trial! During that summer they frequently met for lunch or later in the afternoon, in a bar or at his apartment or sometimes, even, in his office; he had brought in a television to watch while that compelling saga, complete with one blonde damsel in distress (remember Maureen Dean?), unfolded. And though Kathryn wasn't at all happy about the anti-serious direction that American art was taking, and hadn't been since the sixties (Warhol, Pop Art, et cetera), it was a very exhilarating time for American filmmaking, when even Hollywood, then so heavily influenced by European films, especially the French New Wave, was turning out good, brave, and exciting work, and the wonderful film critic Pauline Kael was writing her irreverent and knowing and always anticipated and much-discussed reviews for the *New Yorker* then, too. Also during those years, American and world literature was so vibrant and alive, as feminism's second wave had helped push women writing about women's concerns and women's lives into book form. At last, there was a proliferation of interesting women writers being published, while so many of their male counterparts during that time seemed, somehow simultaneously, to feel the need to assert their masculinity and to prove, especially on television talk shows, which of them was the most macho—as if masculinity had anything whatsoever to do with the quality of writing; Mailer clearly thought it did, and said so. And Luke knew many of these writers, too, women and men, and he and Kathryn discussed all of them—and their work. They admired Cheever—particularly the late novels—and also the then lesser-known Grace Paley, and James Salter; Truman Capote was another favorite of theirs (they tended to prefer the writer's writers)—a terrifically gifted and terribly sad man whose public persona and desperate, often outrageous public appearances were constantly threatening to ruin, and some would say did ruin, his literary reputation. But he wrote such clear and beautiful prose, and he was wickedly funny, too; there are so many memorable *bon mots*, such as his comment that poinsettias were the Bob Goulet of botany. Luke did a mean imitation of him.

And so when Kathryn looked back on those years, as she did now, what she saw in her mind's eye was a *frieze* of her and Luke (as painted by, say, Max Beckmann or Otto Dix) with their heads thrown back, faces slightly red, laughing. Yes, those were largely very happy, even carefree years, as she and Luke traveled a great deal together too—took many trips, usually at least once a year, if not more often, frequently to Europe. While there in the early eighties, she had insisted on taking the train alone to Peter's native Frankfurt. Luke thought she had suddenly gone quite mad!

Though she had never been to Frankfurt, she knew that the city had changed dramatically since Peter's time there: whereas almost all other German cities had tried to reclaim their pre-war appearance after World War II, Frankfurt erected skyscrapers instead. Of course Peter knew of this, had heard about it, but he had not seen it, as he had not been, and said he would not go, back to Germany. And so that day as Kathryn strolled about, she felt as if she was seeing everything *for him*—he would have been appalled. And she almost had to laugh at the irony, reading in a little guidebook, that Frankfurt had, as a result of the many skyscrapers that now punctured the skyline, nicknamed itself *Mainhattan*, using the name of the river that flowed through the city, the Main, to suggest that other famous city, the one that she, Luke and Starling had first coveted and then lived in for so many years.

But mostly she felt very melancholy during that handful of days in Frankfurt, thinking about Peter, missing him intensely—more keenly than she had in years—and yet she was intent on absorbing as much of his birthplace and childhood as she could. She walked to his old neighborhood, across the Main, in Sachsenhauser, and found the street that he and his parents had lived on, Oppenheimst; and then she tried to guess which house was theirs—a silly and senti-mental exercise, since he had never described it to her. It was a rainy

Sunday as she stumbled about the cobblestone streets, which wreaked havoc on her heels, sometimes in tears, indulging herself in memory and fantasy, finally and fully able to grieve the loss of Peter. She had brought with her a little book of Rilke's, *Letters on Cézanne*, and as she walked about that very gloomy and rainy Sunday, she recalled these lines, which she had recently underlined, and which so aptly characterized the day:

> Sounds of rain and bells striking the hour: this makes a pattern, a Sunday pattern. If you didn't know it: this would have to be Sunday. That's how it sounds in my quiet street.

It *was* quiet there.

And she remembered—buttoning her coat against the cold, a button came off and fell between the cracks of the cobblestones. That moment suddenly became very real, very heightened for her, and seemingly all-important: would she stoop down and retrieve the button? Or would she leave it behind in the city of Peter's birth?

No, she thought, *you will claim nothing of me*. And it was then that she realized she was angry at the city, felt that it had betrayed Peter—in so many ways. And so she bent over, pinched the button from between the cracks, put it in her coat pocket, and walked on.

The only other thing she did in Frankfurt, besides sample its famed apple wine, was visit the Goethehaus, more or less in the center of town, which had been carefully rebuilt and faithfully restored after having been destroyed by Allied bombing in the war. Though Peter had renounced his native Germany, his reverence for Goethe had lived on, and while poking about in Goethe's house, she recalled Peter quoting him when he was telling her about his parents and the Nazis, something about our being used to seeing men deride whatever is beyond their sympathies.

She got a chill and suddenly felt very old that day in the Goethehaus, and later, back in her room at the hotel, she decided that she had had enough of Frankfurt. And so late that afternoon she left and took the train back to Paris, back to Luke, feeling so grateful for him— and stayed for the good part of a week and a half.

He had the loan of an acquaintance's apartment on Rue Cler in the Seventh Arrondissement, and he had spent the days Kathryn was in Frankfurt mostly working, or so he told her when she arrived. But now that she was back, Luke said that he would stop working; and since they had both been to Paris many times over the years, they didn't particularly feel the need or the desire to sight-see—they had seen the sights; and so instead they just lived, lived and breathed, like Parisians, and it was glorious.

They would wake up late, one of them would make coffee, and then they would sit and talk and read the newspaper, dipping hunks of bread into the coffee, or sometimes slathering it with butter and *confiture fraise*. They would pad about the apartment and, eventually— often not until well after noon—they would go out, and then they would walk. And walk. And walk—sometimes through the afternoon and into the evening. There was a wonderful open-air market in the neighborhood which they loved to pass through, and where they would sometimes buy fresh meat and produce for dinner—blonde asparagus and veal, *haricots verts* and salmon, or sometimes just a piece of fruit (once, they saw Jeanne Moreau there: how they had loved *Jules et Jim*!). And then they would stroll on, sometimes past the Esplanade des Invalides and toward the Seine, or at other times, down the Avenue de Saxe, toward Montparnasse, often stopping at a sidewalk café along the way, where they would have café crémes and sit and talk and people-watch for hours. Or they would grab a Camembert or paté sandwich from one of the street vendors and continue on their way, eating as they walked.

They also loved spending time in the Marais, strolling along rue de Vielle-du-Temple, or going to that hideous monstrosity of a museum, the Centre Georges Pompidou, where the views from the top floor were priceless. For the cost of a café créme you could sit at a table and look up to the heights of Montmartre and the dome of Sacré Cœur, and west to the Eiffel Tower, or south to Notre Dame; all of this Luke had gleaned from the acquaintance of his whose apartment he and Kathryn were inhabiting. Luke also told her, one day when they were strolling the Marais, that Genet was supposedly living there in a hotel at the time. Often they would stop for a glass or two of wine late in the afternoon, around four, and then an hour or so later, continue on their way.

On one of those afternoons, after Kathryn had had two glasses of wine and not much to eat all day, she decided to tell Luke the reason why she had taken the train to Frankfurt, and all about Peter.

He listened intently, almost bug-eyed, as she told her story.

She waited for him to say something.

I never knew! were the first words out of his mouth. Then he paused and shrugged: I don't know what to say, Kathryn. I'm so happy you had that; he sounds like a wonderful man.

Her eyes were already glazed from the wine, now made all the more watery with tears. Luke was also moved, and he hugged her then, a rare demonstrativeness on his part.

Both she and Luke also relished walking down rue St. Denis as often as they could, where the hookers plied their trade. Because prostitution was tolerated in France, these girls—or she should say women, since some of them were as old as she was, *and even older*—were incredibly brazen, and their openness was refreshing. Against a backdrop of flashy, glittering sex shops advertising "hard shows" and "spectacles", and amid the smells of urine, and cooking oil from the Lebanese food stands, these women—all ages, shapes and sizes, and dressed anywhere from early twentieth-century courtesan to late twentieth-century punk (though the color of choice was most always black)—were all over the street, and not in the shadows. Kathryn remembered that one of them had approached Luke, slithered right up to him as they walked down rue St. Denis; and then when Luke, clearly embarrassed, politely told her that he was not interested and gestured toward Kathryn with his head, and then took her hand as if they were a couple, the prostitute taunted and teased him for another half-block, poking fun at his shyness.

The only remotely touristy thing Kathryn and Luke did during that week-plus was go to Pere-Lachaise Cemetery. She had always wanted to see it, for many reasons, not the least of which was the fact that she knew the Mount Auburn Cemetery, her favorite place in all of greater Boston (Cambridge, actually), had—in the early part of the nineteenth century—been inspired by and based on the Pere-Lachaise. But she and Luke also went because they wanted to see where Oscar Wilde was buried—and they found it, the sphinx monument designed by Jacob Epstein, with the inscription from *The Ballad of Reading Gaol.*

Luke recited the lines aloud:

> And alien tears will fill for him
> Pity's long-broken urn,
> For his mourners will be outcast men,
> And outcasts always mourn.

And suddenly they both knew the reason they were there: *Starling.*

So does that make us outcast men and women? Luke asked wryly.

Kathryn was too moved to respond, and so she just shrugged and smiled. She was thinking about how quickly and easily wounds could be reopened, and about the fact that time did not really heal after all, it just passed: she had experienced as much twice already on this short trip. But it was then and there that she and Luke made the decision to purchase the plot at Woodlawn, and to buy a headstone for Starling—something his family had not done, at least not as far as they knew; so that they could have closure, as well as a place to visit him. And it was then that they also decided to be buried along-side one another.

And as Kathryn and Luke rambled through the streets of Paris, she remarked how similar these days were to their childhood, peram-bulating up and down the neighborhood streets.

All that's missing is the red wagon, Luke said. And then he added: And of course, Starling.

And later, another day, in another café, over another glass or two or three of wine, it was Luke's turn to tell her a secret.

I wish I had been able to do it, he said, almost in a whisper.

At first, she didn't know what he was talking about.

Starling, he said, in response to her obvious confusion. I don't know why I was so intransigent. Then he laughed: It must have been the Priscilla in me—my mother! But then his facial muscles relaxed again and he added, seemingly near tears: Actually, I think it had a lot to do with losing my brother, with Laird: I don't think I've ever really gotten over that. Do you know that his was the first face I remember seeing? Not my mother's, but Laird's. And then after that it just seemed he was always there, by my side—for the first five years of my life anyway. And then he was gone. Luke sighed and shook his head, went silent for a few moments; then he continued: But my point is that my resistance to Starling seems so completely ludicrous to me now; so unnecessary. It was so easy to love him; it could have been so very easy.

I don't know that that's true, Kathryn said, wanting to relieve Luke of any guilt or feeling of regret. Starling was never easy, she added. But then when she looked at Luke, his eyes were watery: he shook his head, put one finger to his lips and mouthed *Sssh*, indicating that he didn't want to talk about it further.

One night, she and Luke had a wonderful dinner in a little restaurant not too far from where they were staying. It was a tiny place—no more than seven or eight tables; it turned out to be a room in the owner's home. She spoke no English whatsoever, and she had this shaggy little black dog that sat at their feet while they ate. Kathryn and Luke were the last to leave, and enough French came back to Kathryn that she was able to carry on a conversation with poor Mme. Bonnerau, who was a widow, and seemed terribly sad and lonely, eager to talk, and very hesitant to let them go. And so Kathryn told her that she, too, was a widow—whether or not this was true, technically speaking, seemed beside the point at the time; she and Luke were just friends, she added, childhood friends, for more than fifty years. And then Luke flirted with Mme. Bonnerau delicately, just enough to flatter her and make her feel better.

Luke was especially delightful company during those years because he seemed, finally, to have come into his own, and to have left so much of the past behind him, to have let go of so much; they both had.

And then he just up and died—quickly, unexpectedly, and prematurely; he was not yet sixty-five. It all came to that, as it will, and as it does; and once again Kathryn was left to try to pick up and go on. But prior to that were the scattered, shattered pieces, Luke's dying itself, which was not pretty. No, he lived for over a week after the stroke, which occurred at work—he had simply slumped over his desk one afternoon, been found by a colleague. Lived in the hospital, that is, which almost seems an oxymoron; and for four of those eight days he was comatose, which was something of a blessing, although those two words together, *comatose* and *blessing*, also seem so very wrong. Kathryn was there with him the entire time, going home only late in the evening when visitor's hours ended, only to return the following morning. And they had some wonderful, memorable conversations during the first three of those four days when Luke was still awake and alert—probably because he knew he was dying.

All in all, I've had a good life, he said, looking not at her but at the sky out the window—as if preparing to become one with it, Kathryn thought later.

I really can't complain, he went on, his gaze now seemingly fixed on that soft blue and white pillowy horizon. And while he seemed proud of that, she also sensed that he wanted very much to reassure her, and for her to know that was how he felt.

And so it was then, as a parting gift, that she finally told him about the book she was and had been writing for so many years; she added that she had always hoped he would be her editor. You just can't die on me, she joked—I need a good editor!

How he loved and laughed at this; but it wasn't long after that he lost consciousness once and for all. And it was then that his colleagues from the office began coming to see him—too late. And his sister Laura, when Kathryn phoned her (their parents were long dead), told Kathryn that she could not come, because her husband was also ill. So Kathryn was the one who was there with Luke, and for Luke—she was his family, as had been the case for so long—holding his hand, talking to him, remembering the past, so much of which they had shared, doing what she could to comfort him, accompanying him as far as she could go on that difficult passage. And then when the end came, Luke somehow managed to do it, to die, in the same way that he had done everything else in his life, which is to say, above all, that he did it with dignity.

And so here she was, now, ten years after that, having gone on, going on. *An old woman alone.* Just this morning she was sitting on the loveseat in the window drinking the one cup of coffee left to her, looking out at the new day and listening to Manhattan's early morning sounds—the grinding of garbage trucks, the whisk of a few cars, car alarms, dog walkers and joggers—when she thought about the fact that most people passing by who looked up and saw her sitting in the lighted window would think: *an old woman alone.* And yes, she supposed she was that—old, or perhaps older—but she was also so much more than that mere summary: she had lived three-quarters of a century; really lived. And she had stories to tell, so many stories. And as she was sitting there, too, she began to think about death—not her own so much, but the deaths of the many that she had loved and lost. And she started to feel sorry for herself, too, and to list them all in her mind, from Uncle Jack on. But then, a mere hour or so later, when the morning light came, brightened the sky, and the first bird sang—after her poached egg and orange juice and wheat toast—she was sitting at the kitchen table reading the morning *Times*, specifically perusing the obituaries, as she had always done, even when she was young (she had long enjoyed seeing how a life is explained, contained, summed-up in a few phrases or paragraphs, seemingly between brackets), when she happened upon the obituary of Seichi Sato, who—so the article said—had survived the bombing of Hiroshima. That, in itself, of course, was of note, but then distinguishing this Seichi Sato even further was the fact that he was thought to have been related by blood to more people killed in the attack on Hiroshima than anyone through any other act of war or atrocity in modern times, a fact compiled and verified by a human rights group.

Kathryn's first response, having read this, was to feel that her earlier self-pity about how many loved ones she had lost was somehow being answered, addressed, responded to—and she was not a religious woman. So she began to think about this Seichi Sato and to wonder how he had borne it, and to wonder, too, about the rest of his life; the article said he had become a Buddhist monk. She began shaming herself for her self-indulgence: how could she?—when this poor man, now dead, had endured so much! And then, for the briefest of moments, the thing that happened to her when she read a novel—or saw a play, or more rarely, a film—with great characters in it, the thing that should happen happened: she transposed their lives, hers and Seichi Sato's, and she thought about the fact that she could not have endured what he had; she somehow knew that instinctively.

And then suddenly, all the faces of those that she had loved and lost came floating into the room, as if suspended—just their heads, nothing more—Luke and Starling, Peter and Richard, Mary Louise and her father and Uncle Jack; and from there she moved on to feeling happy, really and keenly and she would even say very intensely, happy. Happy to be alive this September day in 2001, happy to be sitting there, still able to hear the morning sounds and to enjoy her favorite breakfast, to read the obituaries in the *Times* and think about and remember those she had known and loved.

Oh, Joanie! she suddenly thought, and she wanted so badly to call Joanie right then and there, and to say—what? *I love you? We still have the gift of life?* But she knew that it was too early in the morning and that Joanie would be furious with her. And so gradually, as Kathryn cleared the table and set to work on her book, she turned to musing about the brevity of a human life and how, retrospectively, it is but a flash, an instant—something that takes place between this or that historical event, between this or that much larger and more significant natural phenomenon; and in writing a book in which one is the subject or the main character, she thought, one should really begin as early as possible in the life of that character, so as to seemingly lengthen or extend the life portrayed; to cover more ground; and then, too, to go over that life—those minutes, hours and days—

slowly, and in the greatest of detail, as if with a fine-toothed comb (ah, Proust!). She supposed she was still looking for ways to cheat time, even though she knew it was impossible. Weren't we all?

An old woman alone....
Before too long now, things will become seedier; she won't be able to keep up. Dust will mount then roll across the floor like bolls of wheat over an open prairie. Time will pass and roll over her like the dust, in waves

About the Author

Robin Lippincott

Robin Lippincott is the author of two previous novels and a collection of short stories. His work has also appeared in *The Paris Review*, *Fence*, *The New York Times Book Review*, *The Literary Review*, and many other journals, as well as several anthologies, and he has been awarded fellowships to Yaddo and The MacDowell Colony. He teaches in the MFA Writing Program at Spalding University and at Harvard University. He lives in Cambridge, Massachusetts.

The fonts used in this book are from the Garamond family

The Toby Press publishes fine writing,
available at leading bookstores everywhere. For more
information, please visit www.tobypress.com